More completely made-up endorsements:

"Revisionist history at its worst."
"Disgusting."
"I love it."

> —(um, on reconsideration, perhaps I should not
> have included all these . . .)

Other books by Charley Pearson:

What do you mean, other books? How many you
think I have out there? Everybody's gotta start
somewhere, you know. Cheez, you people are so
greedy.

THE MARIANATED NOTTINGHAM

AND OTHER ABUSES OF THE LANGUAGE

by Charley Pearson

CEP Books

printed by IngramSpark

ME

THIS BOOK IS dedicated to me. *Me*, I tell you. I wrote it. I did all the work. Well, all but the cover and other hard stuff. But I did the punctuation. So I'm dedicating it to myself. And I—

What do you mean, I can't dedicate a book to myself? So what if no one does? I can dedicate my book to . . . wait, put that down. You can't . . . ow!

THIS BOOK IS dedicated to everyone else in the world *except* me. So there, you can now tell everybody you've had a book dedicated to you. I can't, but you can.

So in what universe is this fair? I tell you, things are—

Put that . . . ow!

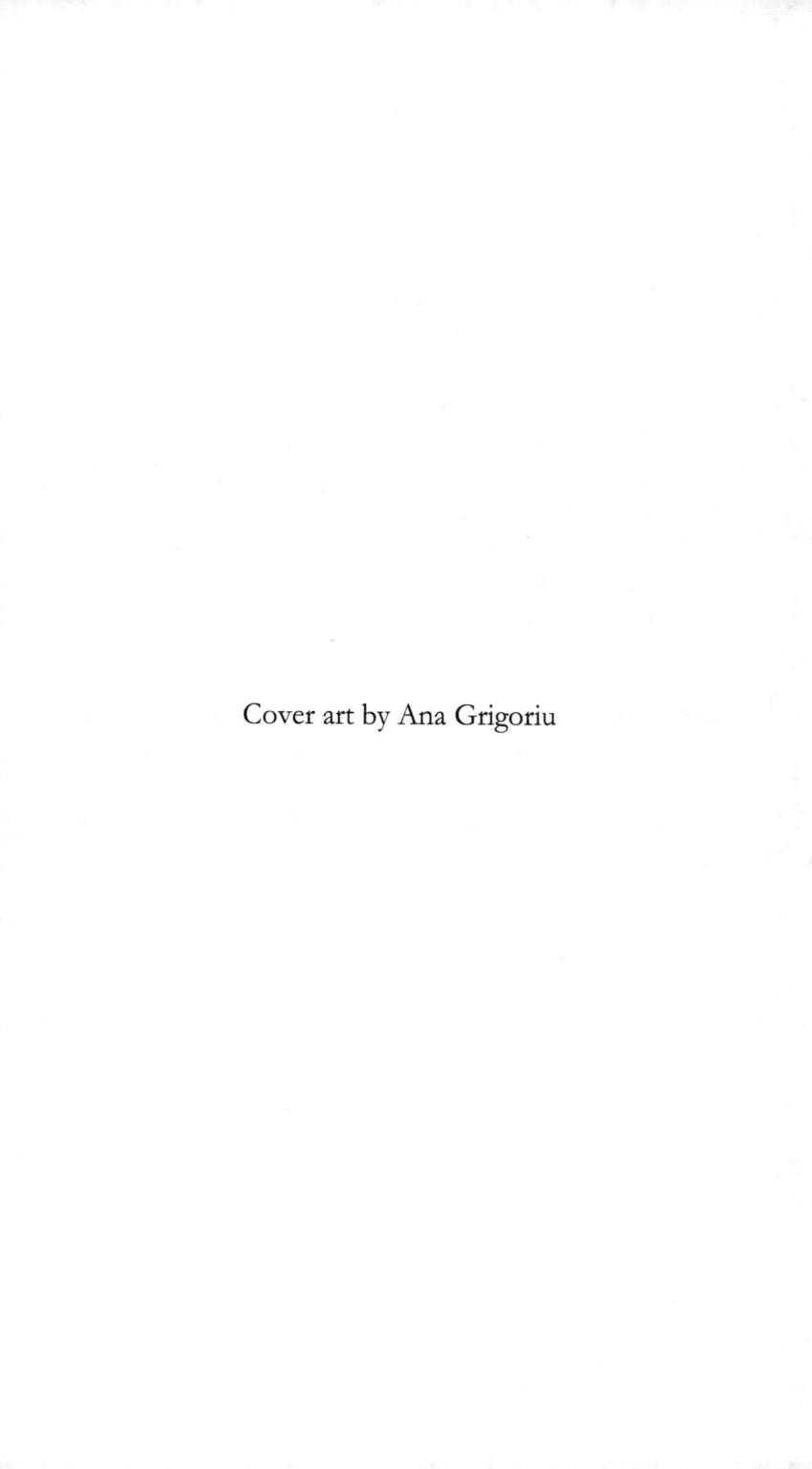

FOREWORD

I was going to call this the "Forward" to see if you're paying attention, but it'd never make it past the editor. Those people have no sense of humor.

Here is where I thank all you gullib—I mean, brilliant folks who bought this book. Or lifted it from a friend, or snuck it out of the library. Whatever, you have saved another from reading it, and thereby performed a humanitarian service. Unless you're reading electrons. Then you haven't done anything useful at all. (heh heh)

Anywho, you are holding one of the grosser misuses of the written word, a collection of humor in non-standard format—screenplays and ballads, with only a few cases of actual prose just to confuse you. That is, a screenplay presented as literature (and I use that term loosely; pretend you're the set designer, and let your mind go wild), and poetry for people who hate poetry—a.k.a. deranged doggerel. Solid meter, strict rhyme, and no redeeming social value.

Of course, you're not really reading this. Nobody reads forewords, they skip to the good stuff. It's just here to make the book longer, so you think you got more for your money. So I can pretty much write anything. Like, your mother's hearing aid is set to filter out everything you say, and you wouldn't know a pomegranate from a—

Oops. Well, there's one in every crowd. Sorry about that bit with your mother.

So you, the single individual actually reading this, if you're not used to reading screenplays, the format becomes as invisible as prose after a while. Just remember it's in present tense; dialogue is indented with the speaker's name capitalized; "INT" and "EXT" indicate new scenes in interior or exterior locations; and if you see "(V.O.)" or "(O.S.)" after a character's name, it means they're speaking as a "voice over" (they're not in the scene, but you hear the voice anyway, like a TV documentary) or they're "off-screen" (they are in the scene, but not visible). And screenplays are always in Courier type, but I didn't figure you wanted to read that. Nor does double-indenting dialogue work well in small books, or in e-book format with selectable font sizes, so I slung most everything to the left. So I guess, really, it doesn't look like a proper screenplay at all. Oh, well.

Now quit wasting time on stupid forewords and turn the page, already.

TABLE OF CONTENTS

(I was going to do this without page numbers)
(after all, you could just look around a little)
(you lazy person)
(but I got talked out of it)
(don'tcha hate it when other people are right?)

(because it's about time someone told the truth
about Robin Hood. I mean, think about it. Here's
this poor sheriff trying to start the world's first
national park to protect the declining deer
population, and redneck Robin Hood hunts. And
don't even get me started on Richard. First he's in
France killing his father to take the throne, then

he's gallivanting off on crusades, then getting kidnapped by Germans, then back to France again. No wonder the English thought he was a good king. He was never around.) (Hey, I warned you not to get me started.) (And by the way, this one is long—a full-length screenplay.)

(This page intentionally blank.)

(Except it's not, because I just wrote that.)

(And that next line, too.)

(So it's not even remotely blank, and . . .)

(never mind)

O'CONNOR'S LAST QUEST

O'Connor's lost glory was quite a sad story,
'Twas making him feel mighty glum,
When townsmen suggested his mettle be tested
By trying a quest that was dumb.

They knew of a dragon who's health, it was flaggin',
And maybe O'Connor could win.
"No way," he first thought. "I couldn't have fought
A dragon back when I was thin."

But then he relented, from boredom consented.
He glanced at the rust on his mail.
His armor, it squeaked, his body, it creaked,
And somehow he knew he might fail.

He shook out the leaves while donning his greaves.
He fell as he mounted but twice.
But then he got down, walked off with a frown,
And wondered how armor got lice.

Returning sans armor, he thought of the farmer
Who'd lent him his dubious steed.
The sway in its back, the weave in its track,
Made riding a challenge indeed.

At last he was ready, resolve almost steady.
"What-Ho!" He was off to the test.
But leagues were a pain, mere three did he gain,
Ere stopping for well-deserved rest.

"Disgraceful," thought he. "I'm just eighty-three;
You'd think I could ride all the night.
Instead I get sore, I'm stiff and what's more,
My bottom's a pitiful sight."

Yet finally he came to the cave with the name:
"Here Gertrude" carved high in the rock.
She had, it was said (a hush full of dread),
A face that could dry up a loch.

With wings that were green, a slime-colored sheen,
And scales that scattered like rain,
She'd seen better days, and in many ways
Was unjustifiably vain.

He knocked 'til she woke, then bravely he spoke.
Quoth he, "I have come here to fight."
She asked him, "But why?" Said he, "I must try
To see if I'm still a great knight."

She snorted and smiled; O'Connor reviled
For trying to get at her hoard.
She then ate his horse, just as a first course,
And picked at her teeth with his sword.

He turned 'round and fled. Right quickly he sped.
He'd lost; 'twas terribly sad.
But then through the ground came a shake and a
sound
That broke rocks, and felled trees, and smelled bad.

For the horse she had swallowed had gas, and it
followed
That dragons, with fiery breath,
Would light off such fare, explode through the air,
And land poor old Gertrude in death.

And so, with great honor, the brave knight O'Connor
Returned from his last famous quest.
And still to this day if you ask him, he'll say,
"How I won? Oh, you'd never have guessed."

MACROHARD #1

FADE IN:

INT. HOTEL BEDROOM - DAY

A pudgy EXECUTIVE kisses a gaudy younger WOMAN in a cheap hotel room. She flops back on the bed, spreading her arms.

The Executive holds up one finger, nodding and smiling. He rips off his tie and sits at the desk in front of his glowing laptop computer screen. He types quickly.

Words appear: MEETING LATE. HOME TOMORROW.

A blue rectangle flashes in the lower corner of the screen, highlighting the word: SEND. He hits another key and grins.

INT. HOUSE

An elegant MATRON marches through a spotless bedroom. She frowns at a faint BUZZING sound. She picks up her cell phone and scans it.

The screen reads: HAVING AFFAIR IN SLEAZY HOTEL.

Her eyes widen in anger.

The picture fades into the logo of MACROHARD: A blacksmith with raised hammer, holding an old-fashioned computer disk with a pair of tongs over an anvil.

NARRATOR (V.O.)
Macrohard—the leading edge in error correction software.

FADE TO BLACK

[You skipped the Foreword, didn't you? Naughty, naughty. Sooooo—INT. and EXT. indicate new scenes in interior or exterior locations, V.O. means "voice over" (like a TV documentary), and O.S. means the speaker is off-screen.]

NOT SO MUCH A CALLING

"THEY TOOK GRAMS."

Myrana spat like a wounded wolverine, her long black ponytail slashing warriors right and left. The Pursuers were too strong, though, and pried her fingers off the sword she'd snitched. A grey-bearded soldier laughed and held it out of reach.

Captain Lanthal pointed at a scrawny body on the ground. "Isn't this your grandmother?"

"Not her." Myrana leapt for the sword, but didn't make it higher than the guard's shoulder. Grown-ups were so darned, well, grown *up*. "My rooster."

"You flagged us down for a chicken thief?" Lanthal traded looks with her sergeant, then glared at Myrana. "You think she's all right?"

"Rooster. Not hen."

"Your grandmother."

"Oh." Myrana gave up on the sword. She went to Grandma and flipped her over. The ancient woman coughed out a couple of feathers. "Great-grandma, really. She's only ninety-seven. She'll last forever."

Lanthal rolled her eyes. "So what happened?"

Myrana hesitated. Clearly, borrowing a weapon and chasing down the thieves herself wasn't in the fates. If she answered the Pursuers' questions, maybe they'd do something.

"A couple came begging. I gave them bread, then Grandma shooed them off. Next thing I know they've got my rooster and Grandma is chasing them with a shovel. And yelling. And tripping over the anvil. I think she landed on Gretchen."

"Another rooster?"

"A hen."

"And the thieves got away."

"Dammit."

"Uh, huh." Lanthal shook her head. "Look, we'll tell the Soltup constabulary, but my troop has bigger bones to break."

Myrana fidgeted while the Pursuers mounted.

Lanthal glanced back. "Vengeance ain't a calling, girl. You leave them alone."

"Yes, ma'am."

"What is your calling, anyway?"

"I'm supposed to live with the sword."

"You mean, by the sword."

Myrana shrugged.

"Don't go bad, girl. A rooster ain't worth it."

Myrana blinked at Lanthal. "I'll try."

Lanthal's mount kicked up dust, and the rest of the Pursuers followed.

Myrana watched them disappear around a hillock. Callings. Everyone had them. And whatever the semantical difference meant, hers was 'with the sword,' not 'by.'

Well, one of hers. No one was supposed to have three, shoved down her diaper by infuriated birth seers degrading each other's predictions. A warrior, or not. A healer, or not. And some confused religious nonsense. Stupid magic, anyway.

Myrana shrugged and helped her Grandma up.

A FEW YEARS later, Grandma succumbed to age, losing a fight to a stag that wanted her vegetables. She'd always said deer were nothing but overgrown rodents. Myrana sold the farm for a pittance and set out to learn what her calling might really be, regardless of those damned birth seers.

Which was why she now found herself kneeling beside a nasty-looking pilgrim bleeding on the road. Fool man thought he had to pray on the limb of a tree, at his age. She tried to patch him up while he fumbled at her empty pouch, attempting to liberate a donation. It did no good. She had no idea how to stop internal bleeding. A stint as apprentice herbalist had taught her little before she accidentally set fire to the laboratory.

The old pilgrim grabbed Myrana's tunic and cast spittle in her ear. "Ka'Rantho Temple," he gasped.

Myrana smiled. "What's a Ka'Rantho Temple?"

"Show respect. Bloodiest god the Warpled Lands ever saw."

"Never heard of him."

The pilgrim grimaced. "No one else. Must believe. Worship."

Myrana snorted. "You got the wrong devotee, pops."

The pilgrim yanked her closer. "Sow's Spine. Foothills."

He went into a spasm, coughing blood. Two minutes later he was still. Myrana reached down and closed his eyes. Then she rocked back on her heals and thought.

The Sow's Spine wasn't safe, what with bandits and Pursuers playing tag. On the other hand, it was only the foothills, and a temple might give her something if she told them of their pilgrim. Maybe he was a priest.

Myrana buried the man, hoping that was the right rite, then led her huge, black, former plow-horse against a tree. She climbed a low branch and lowered her small frame onto the brittle remains of a saddle.

"Come on, Daffodil," she said. The beast didn't move. "Look, it's your name, granite-head."

She nudged the horse with her heels. Nothing happened. She gave it a sharp punch in the withers, followed by a smack with her shortsword. The horse nodded like it finally understood and trotted off, following the rein like it actually had a brain inside the thick bone holding up its eyeballs. Myrana figured that might be getting optimistic.

In three days she found a lonely meadow in the foothills of the Sow's Spine. A decrepit wooden structure leaned against a rocky outcrop at one end of the meadow, not far from the only tree in sight—a scraggly pioneer barely twice her height. Spiky turrets, hardly big enough for a crow to perch on, jutted from each corner of the single-story building, with either carvings or highly imaginative woodworm tracks trailing down their sides.

Myrana chuckled. This, the pilgrim's lost temple? It was gloomy enough.

She stopped chuckling. After all, she'd been hoping for a handout, not an abandoned building. Well, maybe there'd be a trinket left behind.

She dismounted by the tree and rooted through her saddlebags for the hobble. She put it on Daffodil, took two steps, and turned back. The horse was tearing at the bark to get the softer wood inside. She took off the hobble, dragged the recalcitrant equine thirty feet away, and put the hobble back on. She pointed at the ground. "Grass," she said. "Eat that."

The horse moped a bit, but eventually tore into the turf like it had just discovered strawberries. Myrana headed for the building.

She paused outside and pulled a cloth from her belt. Clutching it to her mouth did little to filter the stench. She pushed the door.

The frame collapsed. Inside, ragged gaps in the floor surrounded a few rows of putrefying pews. Myrana decided to try the window at the back.

The shutters dribbled away at her touch, and one tap sent the window frame the way of the door. Myrana eased through the opening. Her foot went through the floorboards and she crashed into a block of wood sitting just inside.

It squished.

"Watch it, Goddess."

Myrana slithered twice, struggling to rise. Her eyes darted around, seeing nothing. "Who's there?" She managed to stand and snatched out her shortsword. "Where are you?"

"At your service, Mistress of . . . whatever you're mistress of. 'Tis I, at your feet." The voice came from below. From the soggy block of wood.

Myrana touched the tip of her blade to the wood. It fizzed. She jerked it back, took the cloth from her face, and rubbed off the sword. Part of the tip was missing.

"You're trapped under—"

"No, Goddess."

"Stop saying that. You're not inside?"

"I am the Altar," said the voice. A section of wall near where the window used to be oozed inward. "Goddess, watch out!"

Myrana leapt aside as the timbers, or what may once have passed for timbers, wandered slowly to the floor and passed through it. She could swear she saw ripples fan out on the remaining floorboards.

"You're the what?"

"I, my dear mistress, am the Altar, your gracious host in this . . . excuse me, watch out for the roof; yes, that's good . . . this great temple of—*duck!*"

"Temple of Duck?" Myrana heard a squishing sound behind her and dove to the side. Another timber collapsed where she had been. She got to her knees, rubbed her head where she'd taken out a pillar, and grabbed up her sword.

"Nice move, Goddess."

"I'm not a frigging goddess, you mouldering pile of fungus food." Myrana jumped up, dove through the hole from the missing window, and staggered away, coughing and spitting.

The Altar behind her started moaning and muttering obscene cantrips. "Are so," it said after a moment. "My chantings went to seed, so the bloody old fart's finally toast."

"What are you—"

"You kill a deity, you take their place." The rest of a side wall fell inward, smashing half the altar. Clouds of slime sprayed through the air. The stench of the temple fell off as Myrana moved away.

"Damn," said the Altar. It sounded like it was chewing a cud. "Look, I haven't much time. You need to get the talisman."

Myrana reached the tree, dropped the useless cloth, and sobbed for breath, leaning on the smooth young bark. It felt good touching wood that didn't sag. How old had that temple been?

Another soggy crash echoed off the rocks beyond.

"I'm serious," came the muffled whine of the Altar. "It's beneath me. Under the floorboards. Or former floorboards."

"I didn't kill anything," said Myrana.

"You came," said the Altar, voice fading as the last piece of roof meandered downward and molded itself to the landscape. "You witnessed the termination of the terminal worshipper. Then your heathen tread desecrated this hallowed hall, your fierce assault mutilated the Temple of Stolen Dreams, last worshipful home of Ka'Rantho, you—"

"The blasted door came off. I fell." Myrana took another breath of relatively fresh air and turned to observe the final descent of walls. This, the highlight of evil nightmares and deranged pilgrims?

"Yeah, well, we . . . just fine . . . barged in . . . retirement benefits . . . ."

Myrana frowned. "Say what?"

Silence. The festering stench lingered, but the former temple had apparently achieved as low a state as it could.

Myrana limped over to her horse. She grabbed her saddlebags and checked the hobble, muttering to herself. Some people had brilliant horses they could give instructions. Disciplined stallions that waited where you left them. She had a hobble.

She sat down, leaned against the tree, and pulled out a stale hunk of bread and moderately fresh piece of sausage. Murdering ancient gods was all well and good, but one had to keep priorities. At least the second seer's nonsense was done with. It couldn't be healing or religion, so only the sword was left.

Bread gone, Myrana took a deep breath and picked up a likely looking stick. She slogged over the remains of the temple, kicking piles of rot to the side. She found only one chunk of slightly decent wood, the core of the altar. She lifted it aside and dug where it had been.

Two hours later, a small pile of valuables lay before her: one small, chipped emerald, a flawed amethyst, and three pieces of pitted bronze jewelry. Lunch money. She could almost smell the cinnamon sweet . . . oh, all right, dammit, the healthy mutton stew. Hacking open the remaining portion of the old altar revealed nothing more than a small, hard stick of heartwood the color of dried blood. Well, reddish brown, anyway. She shrugged and picked it up.

"About time!" yelled the sliver of wood.

Myrana gasped and dropped it. She looked around. The stick was nowhere in sight.

"Look at your hand, O Blind One."

Myrana swallowed and flipped her palm down. The sliver clung to the back of her hand. She pealed it off, but when she tried to pitch it, it clung to her fingers.

"Goodness, aren't we the finicky one?" said the wood. "Why don't you have the talisman yet?"

The wood rasped a couple of times, and Myrana stared at it. Was that a chuckle?

"That's right, Goddess," said the wood. "I am the Altar. Or the heart of it. The rest was just a thick sort of—"

"Get off. Whoever you are."

"Can't. I'm *your* Altar, now."

"My what?"

"For your first temple, the root of your strength. I'll let go and grow when you establish it."

"I'm not a goddess, you benighted piece of kindling." Myrana tried to toss the sliver again. It stuck to her foot, fingers, elbow, or wherever else it liked. "I can't carry you around like this. Let go."

"Just stick me in your pouch," the Altar said. "Easier carrying."

"And will you keep quiet if I wrap you in wool?"

"What? No wool. I break out. Can't sacrifice sheep, either. Sorry."

Myrana glared at it, but somehow that didn't feel satisfying. It didn't have a face to glare at. She scraped the wood on the edge of her pouch, and oddly enough it fell in.

"Now dig up the talisman," came the barely muffled voice.

"With what?" She'd already scraped down to gravel with the stick.

"Use that worthless frog-sticker you're carrying."

"My sword? You're crazy."

"*I'm* crazy? You're the one arguing with a piece of wood."

Myrana threw up her hands, and drew the shortsword.

She had to dig an arrow length deeper, beneath the ancient Altar's bed, before she found a long, narrow, rusted steel box. She pulled it out.

"The old master stole it from a rival a couple millennia ago," said the Altar.

Myrana dropped the box and leapt to her feet. She tore at the bindings on her pouch. "And you want to stick me with whatever it is? Subvert me with your dark god's tools?" The knots seemed glued together, fighting her hands and ripping a fingernail.

"Don't be a dolt. He just gloated and hid it where he thought it'd never be found. He'd have used it if he could figure out anything foul to do with it."

Myrana stopped her fumbling and glanced from the pouch to the box. "Say again?"

"Nine hundred years I had to put up with his smelly, fly-infested sacrifices. You get so tired of people screaming dusk to dawn. Then another five hundred since he got bored and disappeared into the heavens, slowly weakening and losing worshippers. This temple was his last hold on life. And in all that time, never did I see a clean beeswax candle, never a flower, never a stick of incense. Oh, I did so enjoy the smell of incense, ages agone. I can't even remember what it was like, but I know I loved it."

"What are you talking about?" Myrana cleaned the dirt from her blade, shaking her head at the dull nicks. At least the stench was abating.

"I'm sick of serving corrupt gods," said the Altar. "I need a break. I don't really know if it's a talisman or not, but I figure it must be powerful, and I'm hoping you'll be a decent goddess, for at least a millennium or so."

Myrana slowly lowered her hands and opened her pouch. The knots slid apart like oiled silk. She stared at the sliver of heartwood. A shaft of sunlight caught it. It seemed to wink at her.

"You're serious," she said. A freshening breeze flung strands of ebon hair over her shoulder. "You're really . . . ."

"Yup, and you're the Great Goddess . . . er, what should we call you?"

"My name is Myrana."

"No, no, that will never do. You need something grand. Gotta impress the masses. Let's see, I always liked—"

"Forget it," said Myrana. "You can try to make me a useless goddess, but I won't—"

"I've got a great one."

"I'm not changing my name, you idiotic splinter. I don't care what sort of—"

"Will you open the damn box?"

Myrana stopped cold. Hey, she'd won. A first against the moronic stick. She smiled, grabbed the box, and trotted back to the feeble shade of the tree, while the splinter mumbled under its, for lack of a better word, breath. "Now," she said, "this box is pretty weak after all those years underground. How do you suppose . . . ?"

She waited a second, then chimed in when the Altar spoke.

"Use the bloody sword."

The stick harrumphed, a perfect image of sulking. Myrana laughed and pried at the box. The lid squealed a multitude of tones, and she feared it was going to start talking as well. Fortunately, it snapped open and went silent.

So did Myrana. She gazed at the shimmering silver of the most beautiful longsword she had ever seen. Pastoral scenes were lightly etched along the length of the blade, the hilt was wrapped in a strange, luminous hide with that perfect, tacky feel, and the pommel and guard were dusted with a powdering of tiny jewels. Myrana ogled it.

"Oh, rot," said the Altar. "I was hoping it was a wand or something."

Myrana ignored the remark, lifting the sword as if it were a baby. After a long moment, she grabbed the hilt, jumped up, and danced around the tree in the training pattern of the Soltup guards. Or as much as she'd learned before her coins ran out. "It's wonderful. The balance, length . . . ." She stopped after the second time through and opened her pouch to peer in. "Thank you."

The splinter definitely laughed this time. "Yeah, but fancy ironwork won't win you a following. You need charm."

"Thanks a lot."

"Not that kind. You know, enchantment."

"Don't you—"

"I told you, I lost my chantings. Good riddance, too. You wouldn't want to bind sea monsters to attack ships, would you?"

Myrana pulled her head back. "Of course not. I don't like magic, if you must—"

"Or drain the will from crowds, so they hold orgies?"

"Well, that could be kind of—"

"So I need new ones, once you've got disciples to give me potency."

Myrana looked back at the sword. "You seem potent enough. You won't go away."

"That's, uh, not really anything. That's just me."

"Ah," said Myrana, lifting a sheath from the bottom of the box. She mounted the sword on her belt, barely aware of a faint vibration through her boots. "Why don't you totter off to someone else? I can't be a goddess if I don't have a temple or worshippers, right?"

"You get a grace period."

"Grace? Like what? You hang around till I die off, if I refuse to tell anyone or build you a frigging house?"

"It's variable," said the Altar defensively. "Could be a couple centuries or so."

Myrana stared at her pouch. "You're going to keep me alive for two hundred years, getting arthritis, going blind, losing the odd foot and all my teeth, for your god-forsaken godhood?"

"Actually, it's goddessness. No, wait. Deityism? Er—"

"Shut up. Just shut up."

Myrana removed Daffodil's hobble, and froze. Vibrations. She glanced at her pouch. "Horses. You bringing someone?"

The vibrations turned into a roar. Myrana barely had a foot in the stirrup when a Pursuer came pounding over the crest of the hill, huddled low in the saddle. His mount stumbled and collapsed halfway to the tree. The soldier rolled free and crouched on the ground, holding his belly.

Myrana raced toward him, but he pointed at the mare. "Help . . . ." He gestured again. "She spooked with an arrow up her ass."

Myrana hesitated, then checked the wheezing animal. It had an arrow in its flank, a shattered leg from the fall, and it sounded like it had run itself to death. Myrana looked at the man and shook her head.

He grimaced. "End it."

Myrana nodded. Poor thing. More soldiers poured over the ridge, but that could wait. She laid her new blade along the artery in the horse's neck, and gave a clean slice.

The next thing she knew, the horse was clambering to its feet, snorting with energy, the arrow was laying on the ground, and the stick in her pouch was humming the most out-of-tune ditty she'd ever heard.

"Come, Acelot," said the soldier. "Come to Jackers."

The animal ambled over, then held still while he clung to a stirrup and tried to rise.

"My god," said Myrana, gaping at the horse. "It obeys." She glanced at Daffodil, meandering halfway across the glen, then realized she and Jackers were surrounded by other Pursuers.

"And—it's healed," said Captain Lanthal.

Myrana whipped her head around. It was the same Captain she'd met years back. "Oh, yeah. That." She looked down as a faint glow faded from her sword. She whisked it behind her leg, but the damage was done. Most of the soldiers were staring at her. "It wasn't hurt that . . . badly . . . ?"

Another soldier tried to help Jackers. When they pulled his jerkin free, his guts were showing. Lanthal grimaced and looked at Myrana.

"He needs the mercy stroke. Would you?"

Myrana shuddered. She looked at her blade. Her talisman. The humming from the pouch was deafening, with faint chanting about magnified desires. No one else seemed to hear.

Jackers had the nerve to smile. He tilted his head to the side, stretching the artery. Myrana clenched her teeth.

Two minutes later, Jackers lay gasping, wounds healed, gazing adoringly at Myrana. She didn't see.

She stared at the fading glow on her blade. Then she tilted her head, her eyes went huge, and she tore at the pouch. *"No, you slimy wood pulp. I won't. I'm not."*

"You are," yelled the Altar. Myrana's pouch flew open and the strip of wood soared past her grasping hand, pulsing scarlet in the deepening twilight. "The Great Goddess . . . uh, Myrana. She can heal blight, and plague, and bad dice rolling. Plant me here. I'll be the best Altar you ever—"

Myrana sprang up, snatched it out of the air, and squeezed as hard as she could. "I thought you only talked to me."

"Mrphmph. Never said that. Ouch."

Myrana cupped the splinter in one hand and pressed the sword against it. "We're leaving."

"No, we build," said Jackers. "Leave it here. Plant the Altar."

Myrana glared. He flinched.

Captain Lanthal laughed. "Can't stop people believing things. But I'd watch it with the dice rolling."

"I do not—"

"You really a goddess?"

Myrana hesitated, looking from the stick to the horse to Jackers. "I suppose so." She let out a breath. "Either that or I've got one hell of an Altar-ego."

Lanthal laughed again. She made to slap Myrana on the shoulder, then stopped at the last second. "Is it all right to touch you?"

Myrana looked exasperated, then thoughtful. She eyed the stick. "Don't you dare," she said. "You want to invent a chanting, you figure when someone's a threat, and damn well leave off when they're not."

"I could . . . all right, no sparks. No throwing. Lousy way to treat a goddess, though. No respect. I remember—"

"Stifle it." Myrana looked at Jackers. "No temple. No worship."

Jackers glanced at Lanthal, bobbed his head at Myrana, and backed away.

Lanthal grinned. "Nice. Don't suppose you could fix up something short of lethal?" She gestured toward other wounded Pursuers.

Myrana looked at her sword, then scraped it on the splinter. "How about it? You can read this now, yes? How's it work?"

"Oh, fine, insult me, ignore me, threaten me, then expect me to—ouch! All right. Just chop—"

"No," said Myrana. "I won't scare them to death. Make it easier."

"Don't have to. But it's more impressive. Ow! Fine. Just match the wound. A scratch to heal a scratch."

"Much better."

"You won't get many converts that way."

"I told you—"

"You got no sense of showmanship."

"Thank you." Myrana looked at the Captain. "Lead on." She lowered the sword and held the Altar up to her face. "And you keep quiet. Mind-to-mind. Understand?"

"But think how much they believe—"

She tickled the sliver with the tip of the blade. After a moment, she smiled. "Better." She dropped it in her pouch and yanked it tight. Then she followed the Captain, telling her about the Ka'Rantho Temple and playing curer.

Next morning, Lanthal kept Daffodil from eating the rein while Myrana mounted.

"Remember," said Lanthal, "that stick of yours could be right. You may need a few believers to keep your powers up. And mending ain't a bad calling."

Myrana sighed. "It's not so much a calling as a summons. With armed escort. But at least I finally have a trade." Then she looked startled and glanced at her pouch. "All right, fine. All three birth seers were correct. Now shut up. And yes, I'll get you some incense."

Lanthal looked down and hid her mouth, coughing. Myrana turned to go.

"Good luck, kid," said Lanthal. "Won't be easy, learning godhood."

"Actually," said Myrana, "I think it's goddesshood. No, wait, um . . . ."

MACROHARD #2

FADE IN:

INT. KID'S BEDROOM - NIGHT

A KID slams his joystick forward, staring at a computer screen. One hand darts forward and jabs at the keys.

The screen flashes brilliant bursts of red, yellow, magenta, destroying the game image.

And then it goes blank.

>   KID
>   Don't tell me . . .

The screen hisses. Speckles of white pop and sizzle. A spectral shape, a GHOST, spirals around the monitor, unseen by the Kid. It dives into an input/output port.

INT. INSIDE COMPUTER

The Ghost sails across the motherboard to a gaudy rainbow-colored chip and flickers around it. Lights flash green, red, and blue as the Ghost passes through the chip.

Close-up on the chip: "Ghost Muster 1-A."

INT. KID'S BEDROOM

The screen flashes turquoise, blanks, and words march one letter at a time across the center:

"Clean Your Room"

The Kid twists to yell over his shoulder.

> KID
> Dad. Mom's back.

The picture fades into the logo of MACROHARD: A blacksmith with raised hammer, holding an old-fashioned computer disk with a pair of tongs over an anvil.

> NARRATOR (V.O.)
> Macrohard—the leading edge in paranormal communications technology.

FADE TO BLACK

TOOTHPASTE

FADE IN:

INT. BATHROOM - DAY

A TEENAGE BOY stumbles up to the sink, squinting and inspecting one eye in the mirror, and brushing an inch-long eyelash. His other eye is normal.

He blinks and shakes his head, green Mohawk-hair quivering and three left earrings jingling. He's got a tattoo on one cheek, and the right half of a Fu Manchu beard. He pulls his lips back and glances at his teeth.

He grabs a tube of toothpaste from a basket on the sink and squeezes out a glob of white. He stares at it. He shakes it into the sink.

> ANNOUNCER (V.O.)
> Tired of the same old color?

The Teenager snatches another tube, squeezes out green, and tosses down the tube. He grabs another, gets stripes, and pitches it. He inspects his teeth again.

> ANNOUNCER (V.O.)
> Just white. No matter the paste, the teeth don't change.

The Teenager rubs his tongue over his front teeth, takes a breath, then charges out the door.

He returns with a bag and pulls out a black tube bearing the words "OLD MASTERS."

ANNOUNCER (V.O.)
Why look like everyone else?

The Teenager pinches the tube. Black paste oozes onto his brush. He attacks his teeth.

ANNOUNCER (V.O.)
The Old Masters knew fine art. The value of shade and shadow.

Black foam obscures the Teenager's mouth, dribbling down his chin.

ANNOUNCER (V.O.)
The subtleties of darkness.

The Teenager tosses down the black tube and his brush. He rinses.

ANNOUNCER (V.O.)
Now Old Masters toothpaste gives you the flavor of their work.

The Teenager leans over and spits a thick black stream into the white sink. He closes his mouth, stands, and looks straight in the mirror. He pulls back his lips.

Painted across his teeth is a brilliant mural, a pastoral scene with trees and stream on the bottom; clouds, birds, and hills above. Birds CHIRP in the background.

ANNOUNCER (V.O.)
What, you thought they'd be all black?

The image fades to a picture of a black tube of toothpaste, the name OLD MASTERS in shiny, grayish letters.

ANNOUNCER (V.O.)
Old Masters. When you're ready for something *really* different.

FADE TO BLACK

DEAD-MAN MALONE

The northwoods is slimy, the autumn wind say,
With mildew and mold-rotty spore.
But oncet a fortnight it's bugger gone fey,
With sticky saliva and gore.

The northwoods is creepy, come new moon or full,
And brave be the soul on 'is own,
For trees they be dyin' like worm-eaten skull,
And roamin' goes dead-man Malone.

'Twas dashing of figure, Malone in 'is prime,
Disdainful of things sacramental.
At eighty, unshriven, and undead betime,
Now suck he the life elemental.

The northwoods is thick with the burden of trees,
But now it's a-comin' more bleak,
For legions stand leafless and gaunt in the breeze,
And maples is 'specially weak.

The sugar-sap harvesters weep as they work,
Their crop is gone feeble and sour.
Malone done 'is suckin', now silent he lurk.
He'll strike in a fortnightly hour.

The northwoods cain't heal till it's rid o' that pest,
That foul-sucking octogenarian.
So meantime we's stuck with the scourge of our
guest—
A vampire gone vegetarian.

And *finally*, the main event.
(Yeah, yeah, I know. About friggin' time . . . .)

THE MARIANATED NOTTINGHAM

FADE IN:

EXT. SOGGY FIELD - A.D. 1189 - DAY

Globs of mud fly from the hooves of armored WAR STEEDS. RICHARD of England and PHILIP of France look around as they ride. Six GUARDS follow.

Ahead of them, the field is strewn with CORPSES of soldiers, NOISY CROWS, and French SOLDIERS looting the dead.

A SKINNY SOLDIER holds a brownish roll. He CLANGS it against his helmet, then tries to bite it.

A few WHORES slog through the filth: an ANCIENT one shields her eyes; a MIDDLE-AGED one holds her nose; and a BEAUTIFUL one reads a small book.

> ANCIENT WHORE
> Post battle special, half price.

> MIDDLE-AGED WHORE
> Third price. No, five-sixteenths. Cor, what's that in francs?

The Ancient Whore sniffs. A MUSTACHED SOLDIER studies the Middle-aged Whore. She lifts her skirt; he waves her off.

> BEAUTIFUL WHORE
> Full price. Every day the same.

The Skinny Soldier looks at the Beautiful Whore, then catches sight of the approaching riders.

> SKINNY SOLDIER
> Hail, Philip of France. Hail . . .

He whispers with the Mustached Soldier.

> SKINNY SOLDIER
> . . . Richard.

Richard tosses him a salute and splashes to a stop before the whores. Philip blindly gallops on; half the Guards try to follow, blocked by the half stopping with Richard. Ineptitude versus pandemonium.

> RICHARD
> What, ho, lovely maidens. Be ye seers, to grace my victory with brave omens?

The Guards crudely chuckle while sorting themselves out. Philip stops, looking around. The three Whores glance at each other. The Ancient Whore throws out her arms.

> ANCIENT WHORE
> Boil, toil, royal soil.

The Middle-aged Whore grins. Philip heads back.

MIDDLE-AGED WHORE
By the pricking of my nose, parenticidal power
grows.

The Beautiful Whore shuts her book and weaves back
and forth, eyes shut. Philip rejoins the group. The
Guards finally manage to get in line.

BEAUTIFUL WHORE
Beware, Richard. Beware the Ides of March. No,
wait, it's a little later. Call it the twenty-sixth.

The Whores laugh raucously. Richard looks miffed
and reaches for his sword, but Philip grabs his arm
and points toward a village in the distance. They ride.

INT. TRADESMAN'S HOUSE - LATER

In a poorly furnished bedroom, the body of KING
HENRY lies in state, a crown on his head. A MAID
adjusts a crudely drawn sign at the head of the bed
reading, "HENRY II, RIP."

Richard and Philip stomp into the room and glare at
the corpse. The Maid curtsies.

RICHARD
So long, Pop.

Richard slaps the King's boot. The middle finger of
the King's hand shoots up, a rude gesture aimed at
Richard.

The Maid gasps and shoves the finger down; it
bounces up. She pumps it down twice like a water
pump. Blood spurts from Henry's mouth. The Maid
runs out shrieking.

Richard draws his blade and lays it against the King's hand. The finger sags down. Richard snorts and raises his sword.

>   RICHARD
> I hereby claim the Plantagenet dominions formerly held by Henry the Second, including England, Anjou, Normandy, Brittany—

Philip shrugs and grabs a huge bible from a shelf.

>   RICHARD
> —Wales, Scotland, Ireland—

Philip looks up, halfway through the old testament.

>   PHILIP
> You don't—

>   RICHARD
> —Aquitaine, Gascony, that funny little place to the east . . .

Philip thumbs the pages faster, looking upset.

>   PHILIP
> Quercy. But I—

>   RICHARD
> Thank you. Perigord, La Marche, Agenais—

Philip slams the book and steps toward him, gritting his teeth. Richard pauses; he shrugs.

>   RICHARD
> And . . . some other stuff.

Richard lowers his sword. Philip looks slightly mollified, and tosses the book aside.

>   PHILIP
> So, you've defeated your father and taken the throne. What're you going to do next?

Richard draws himself up.

>   RICHARD
> I'm going to Jerusalem.

Philip grins. They high-five each other.

>   RICHARD and PHILIP
> It's Crusade Time!

EXT. ENGLISH VILLAGE - DAY

An officious OFFICIAL stands on a log and rants at a small crowd of PEASANTS.

>   OFFICIAL
> Crusade! Rally for Richard! Destroy the Infidel!

>   PEASANT ONE
> What's an infidel?

>   OFFICIAL
> Arabs and things. You know. Semitics.

>   PEASANT ONE
> Semi-ticks?

>   PEASANT TWO
> Half as bad as ticks.

PEASANT ONE
I got a tick.

PEASANT ONE searches for his tick. The Official looks upset.

OFFICIAL
No. Foreigners. They live way south.

PEASANT TWO
What, like London?

PEASANT THREE
More like France.

PEASANT ONE
Found it.

The Peasants admire Peasant One's tick.

OFFICIAL
We must drive them out. With Richard's Crusade.

PEASANT TWO
Oh, like a riot.

PEASANT THREE
I like riots.

PEASANT ONE
Riot for Richard!

PEASANT TWO
Christians for the Crusade!

PEASANT THREE
Stone the bloody frogs.

The Peasants wander off. The Official throws up his hands. CHANCELLOR LONGCHAMP comes out of an inn behind him.

> OFFICIAL
> Chancellor Longchamp, they're after French. That's us. More or less.

> LONGCHAMP
> Support Richard. Enough.

> OFFICIAL
> But a crusade. The taxes—

> LONGCHAMP
> Wait. Thinking. Got it.

> OFFICIAL
> What?

> LONGCHAMP
> Sheriffs collect taxes. King Richard clean.

> OFFICIAL
> Sheriffs?

Longchamp grins, brushes lint off his fancy coat, and enters the inn. The Official looks dubious and follows him. In the background, the Peasants CHANT about rioting.

EXT. OUTSIDE ENGLISH VILLAGE - DAY

CHILDREN march and CHANT outside a village, led by seventeen-year-old ROBIN HOOD. More Children join them.

            CHILDREN
        (slightly in unison)
    Riot for Richard! Christians for the Crusade!

They reach a copse.

            FAT BOY
    Infidels out.

            FILTHY GIRL
    Death to alien dogs.

A CAT darts in front of them and races up a tree.
Robin points.

            ROBIN
    And cats!

The Children pick up stones and heave them at the
tree. None come close to the Cat. The Cat HISSES
and claws.

A twenty-year-old MINOR NOBLE rides up—the
man destined to become the SHERIFF OF
NOTTINGHAM. He has a brace of rabbits and a
pheasant slung at the back of his horse. Dirt and
sweat coat his jerkin.

Nottingham draws his sword and defends the Cat,
swatting rocks away like baseballs.

            NOTTINGHAM
    What are you doing?

            FAT BOY
    It's a French cat.

Robin sneers and starts another chant.

        ROBIN AND CHILDREN
    Riot for Richard! Christians for the Crusade!

Robin throws another stone at the Cat. Nottingham growls and spurs his horse, scattering the Children.

Nottingham rides back to the tree. He removes a gauntlet, reaches up, and grimaces. The Cat leaps on his arm and struts to his shoulder, one paw on his neck.

Nottingham smiles in relief, relaxing. The Cat digs in claws and leaps to the ground. Nottingham YELPS.

INT. JOHN'S CASTLE STUDY - DAY

COUNT JOHN writes music at a desk in a small, private study. He YELPS and crosses out a measure. He resumes his composition, HUMMING more or less in tune.

His servant COGSWORTH enters.

        COGSWORTH
    Excuse me, Prince John.

        JOHN
    Count.

        COGSWORTH
    One, two—

        JOHN
    No, you spitwad. My title. Count John.

Cogsworth sniffs.

>COGSWORTH
>The king's brother should . . . .

John eyes him briefly.

>COGSWORTH
>Very well, "Count." Your conspiracy is in the drawing room.

John throws down his quill.

>JOHN
>Again?

>COGSWORTH
>Shall I see them in?

>JOHN
>Don't bring them here.

John heads for the door.

INT. CASTLE DRAWING ROOM

John stomps into a room filled with ARTISTS sketching at easels in a variety of styles. One paints a Salvador Dali knight, dripping over the edge of a cliff. Three BARONS in brightly-colored tunics huddle in the center.

>JOHN
>Good Barons, must we do this?

>BLUE BARON
>Necessary.

RED BARON
Essential.

GREEN BARON
Probably.

Red and Blue cast a dirty look at the Green Baron. He twitches. All the Artists start drawing caricatures of the group, as the Barons and John move to a corner.

JOHN
Richard's crowned barely a month—

BLUE BARON
Don't matter. You're the heir.

RED BARON
Gotta plot. This is the twelfth century.

GREEN BARON
Actually, almost the thirteenth.

The other Barons glare at the Green one. He looks aside, and frowns at a caricature being drawn—the Red Baron in a Fokker Triplane. Blue and Red look back at John.

BLUE BARON
He's raised the taxes again.

JOHN
Already?

RED BARON
And we've proof he killed Henry.

John's eyes flash.

JOHN
You didn't know our father. I'm sure Richard had a perfectly good reason.

He stalks away. The Blue and Red Barons pout.

GREEN BARON
He could be right.

Blue and Red turn on Green, beating him with their hats.

EXT. HOVEL IN WOODS - DAY

Nottingham arrives at a small hovel. Wretched old MRS. HOOD beats on a rug. She peers up at Nottingham.

MRS. HOOD
You after my daughter again, you French faggot?

Nottingham pauses, then reaches back and gets the pheasant dangling from his saddle.

NOTTINGHAM
It's a long time since 1066, Mrs. Hood.

He hands her the pheasant.

NOTTINGHAM
We speak English now.

Mrs. Hood snatches the bird and eyes it suspiciously.

MRS. HOOD
Marian ain't here. She run off with a *man*.

He stares; she cackles in glee.

> NOTTINGHAM
> But who . . . ?

> MRS. HOOD
> Anyone but a tick-loving Frog.

Nottingham takes a breath and turns to go—and catches a glimpse of Robin. Robin grins, then CROAKS and hops around by the corner of the hut.

Nottingham feints toward Robin. Robin YELPS and scurries away, knocking over a rack of tools. Rakes and shovels CRASH.

INT. CASTLE - DAY

Richard kicks an array of pikes and halberds. They CRASH. Longchamp flinches. Richard grabs a sword and SMASHES the flat of it against a table. The sword shatters.

> RICHARD
> That's what I mean. I can't kill with crap.

> LONGCHAMP
> Richard, Sire, best smiths—

> RICHARD
> —in France. Tell the Arabs that.

Richard grabs Longchamp's surcoat.

> RICHARD
> I want English bows. French armor. And Spanish swords.

He thrusts Longchamp away and looks back at the
table of weapons.

          LONGCHAMP
Cost. Taxes.

Richard shoves over the table. Weapons CLATTER.

          RICHARD
I don't care. They're English.

Longchamp bows himself a quick exit.

EXT. VILLAGE - DAY

Count John and four GUARDS ride up to confused
PEASANTS rioting at the edge of town. The
Peasants YELL and try to tie up a DOG. Nottingham
struggles to free it.

A FAMILY huddles just beyond, in front of their
house, CRYING and BEGGING for mercy.

John closes his eyes and shakes his head, but when he
opens them the scene hasn't changed. He waves his
Guards forward. They break up the crowd of
Peasants. Nottingham takes the Dog.

          JOHN
I don't want to hear this, do I?

The Peasants shuffle their feet, MUMBLING.
Nottingham looks at John, but John puts a hand out,
silencing him.

          PEASANT ONE
It's orders, Count John.

PEASANT TWO
Well, policy.

JOHN
Whose?

PEASANT ONE
King Richard's.

PEASANT TWO
We're supposed to kill alien dogs.

Robin waves a bow from the back of the mob.

ROBIN
And cats.

Nottingham glares at Robin. A voice comes from the side.

PEASANT THREE
And parakeets.

The mob looks baffled.

PEASANT ONE
What's a parakeet?

Peasant Three pushes his way forward.

PEASANT THREE
It's this noisy little bird from South America. Chirp, chirp, all day long. Can't shut 'em up. They just—

JOHN
America hasn't been discovered yet.

> PEASANT THREE
> Oh. Right, then. Make that canaries.

John looks at him a moment while the Peasants MUMBLE about canaries. Then John glances at the huddled Family and the Dog struggling in Nottingham's arms.

> JOHN
> And you think my brother is behind this? Killing foreign . . . dogs?

The Peasants avoid looking at each other.

> PEASANT ONE
> Must be.

> PEASANT TWO
> What I heard.

> PEASANT THREE
> He ain't stopped us.

John grinds his teeth.

> JOHN
> Then I will.

He signals and his Guards scatter the mob of Peasants.

Nottingham releases the dog to the grateful Family.

> NOTTINGHAM
> Watch yourselves. It's not a big step from killing your pets, to killing . . .

He glares. They quiver. He jabs his finger to the side.

> **NOTTINGHAM**
> . . . your livestock.

They MOAN in fear. A scraggly COW beside the hut looks up.

> **COW**
> Moo?

John rides over to Nottingham.

> **JOHN**
> I should make you sheriff. Right stuff, and all that. What shire is this?

> **NOTTINGHAM**
> Nottinghamshire, m'lord. But I don't—

> **JOHN**
> Excellent. I'll speak to Chancellor Longchamp.

He wheels his horse about. His Guards surround him as he rides off. A few Peasants linger, waving fists at John. Nottingham shakes his head and disappears the other way.

> **PEASANT ONE**
> Vile oppressor.

> **ROBIN**
> What's an oppressor?

> **PEASANT TWO**
> Vile French oppressor.

ROBIN
What's an oppressor?

PEASANT THREE
Vile French parakeet oppressor.

The others look at Peasant Three.

PEASANT THREE
Fine. Canaries.

EXT. NOTTINGHAM'S ESTATE - DAY

A CANARY CHIRPS in a cage. Nottingham's small
MANOR is practically obscured by scores of cages, all
large, housing OWLS, FERRETS, SNAKES,
MONKEYS, a LEOPARD, and a RAVEN. A
PYGMY HIPPO snorts in a pen.

Nottingham tosses a dead rabbit to the leopard and
carts a sack of grain to the pygmy hippo. He looks at
a snake swaying in a wicker basket.

NOTTINGHAM
I said no. You'll lose your figure.

Crows CRY out. Nottingham looks up and sees a
gilded CARRIAGE approach, bearing the image of a
huge YELLOW ROSE. A dozen grim GUARDS ride
escort. Nottingham watches a moment, then carts his
animal food to a shed.

As Nottingham emerges, the carriage draws to a stop.
The Guards fan out and Longchamp steps down,
another yellow rose emblazoned on his surcoat.
Nottingham raises an eyebrow and kneels.

NOTTINGHAM
My lord Chancellor.

LONGCHAMP
Fine.

Nottingham starts to get up.

LONGCHAMP
No, kneeling. Stay.

Nottingham kneels again, looking exasperated. The caged Raven bobs its head.

RAVEN
Pretty boy. Pretty.

Longchamp looks around for the voice, then stumbles, staring at all the animals.

NOTTINGHAM
May I help your lordship?

RAVEN
Never. More never.

Longchamp glares at the bird. A Guard throws a rock and smashes open its cage. The Raven flies to the manor roof.

NOTTINGHAM
Leave the poor bird alone.

RAVEN
Po' bird. Po'.

> LONGCHAMP

Count John—

> NOTTINGHAM

I won't be a sheriff. Not now. You've turned them into tax collectors.

Longchamp slowly turns his gaze to Nottingham.

> LONGCHAMP

Not support crusade?

All Longchamp's Guards swivel their eyes toward Nottingham.

> NOTTINGHAM

The church likes it. I support the church.

> LONGCHAMP

Relish opportunity. Aid King. Holy quest.

> NOTTINGHAM

No. He asks too much. His taxes—

Longchamp twitches his nose. A Guard slugs Nottingham; he sprawls in the mud, then pushes himself up and stands.

> NOTTINGHAM

There's nothing you could do—

Longchamp looks over at the Pygmy Hippo.

> LONGCHAMP

Piggy thing. Edible?

Nottingham blinks. Longchamp signals his Guards. Three wade into the pygmy hippo pen and grab the beast. A COARSE GUARD laughs and pulls a giant fork from his sleeve.

                    NOTTINGHAM
You wouldn't.

                    LONGCHAMP
Be sheriff.

                    NOTTINGHAM
Never.

                    RAVEN
Never.

The Coarse Guard steps behind the Pygmy Hippo, licking lips.

                    NOTTINGHAM
You couldn't.

                    LONGCHAMP
Collect taxes.

                    COARSE GUARD
          (upper-crust accent)
This is a young hippopotamus amphibius, then? Should it perhaps be cooked?

The Guards laugh. The Pygmy Hippo struggles.

                    LONGCHAMP
Safe. Germ theory not invented.

> NOTTINGHAM
> Please.

The Coarse Guard raises fork on high. Longchamp sneers.

> NOTTINGHAM
> All right. I'll do it.

The Coarse Guard swivels his head, disappointment rippling across his face. Longchamp turns back to Nottingham.

Nottingham glances from the Guards to Longchamp, then goes down on one knee. Longchamp lets out a breath, reaches into a capacious pocket in his coat, and pulls out a silver chain.

The chain bears a huge silver "S" medallion that barely skirts trademark violation for the "Superman" logo. Longchamp places it over Nottingham's head, the "S" centered on his chest.

> LONGCHAMP
> By power vested, appoint Sheriff, Nottingham. Henceforth known . . . . What name?

> NOTTINGHAM
> Llewelyn, your lordship.

> LONGCHAMP
> Clue . . . ?

> NOTTINGHAM
> It's Welsh.

LONGCHAMP
Feminine.

NOTTINGHAM
Not for several hundred years.

Longchamp frowns.

LONGCHAMP
Name Nottingham.

He waves a haphazard cross in the air and gets in his carriage. The Guards let up the Pygmy Hippo; the Coarse Guard slips the fork up his sleeve; the Guards fall in behind the carriage. Nottingham stands.

LONGCHAMP
Collect. Lots. Big zoo.

He laughs as the carriage pulls away. The Pygmy Hippo lets out a FART. A Monkey gives the carriage a RASPBERRY.

RAVEN
Taxes. Yellow rose of taxes.

NOTTINGHAM
Oh, shut up.

EXT. HOVEL IN WOODS - DAY

Nottingham stops his horse in the brush twenty feet from the hovel. Mrs. Hood is not in sight.

Robin sits on a fence, waving a pitchfork in the air, singing in a perfect tenor.

> ROBIN
> My agent says my blade is true,
> At bow I have no peer,
> I'm brave and daring semi-through.
> Oh peasant, lend an ear.
>
> So I decline my sword to drill,
> Or shoot a single shaft.
> Good PR beats authentic skill,
> And working hard is daft.

MARIAN slips between the trees, grabs Nottingham's arm, and drags him off his horse. Before he can react she has him pinned to the ground, a knife at his throat.

He freezes. She leans forward slowly, and kisses him.

> NOTTINGHAM
> Your mother said you ran off with some man.

She snorts and puts the knife away. Nottingham sits up.

> MARIAN
> Chasing a pig thief.

Nottingham grins and attacks her, tickling unmercifully. Robin approaches.

> ROBIN
> Marian, you know he's sheriff now?

They break, covered with leaves. Nottingham glares at Robin. Marian hesitates, looks from one to the other, then shrugs, brushing a twig from her hair.

MARIAN
Nice job. And still consorting with us peasants, m'lord?

Nottingham looks exasperated. Mrs. Hood walks up.

MRS. HOOD
It's not that. Sheriffs collect taxes now. And they just doubled them.

Her eyes burn holes in Nottingham. Marian backs away.

MARIAN
You take people's homes?

ROBIN
Right up your alley, Frog.

MRS. HOOD
(to Marian)
Don't worry, you little trollop. If he kicks me out, he'll find you a brothel.

MARIAN
Mother!

Nottingham stands. He tries to help Marian, but she hisses at him, backs some more, and stands on her own.

NOTTINGHAM
Look, I—

MARIAN
Get out.

He blinks. She heads for the hovel. He follows. Robin runs for the shed.

> NOTTINGHAM
> Marian, I—

> MARIAN
> I can't believe she was right. Just another thieving French invader.

She steps into the hovel, grabs a crossbow off the inside wall, and glares at Nottingham from the doorway. He stops.

> MARIAN
> Tax collector.

Robin runs up with a bow, nocking an arrow.

> ROBIN
> Leave now. Or else.

He draws the bow, most of the way, and starts quivering. Nottingham swivels to face him, face gone red.

> NOTTINGHAM
> How dare you?

Robin draws further.

> NOTTINGHAM
> No Englishman treats a bow like that. Draw the string to your cheek. Stiffen your left arm. No, rotate it, or you'll take your elbow off when you shoot.

Robin frowns and tries to improve his draw, quaking like a raw recruit.

> NOTTINGHAM
> And do some push-ups. You're the flimsiest archer I ever saw.

Robin accidently fires. The arrow misses Nottingham by several feet and just misses a low-flying bird.

> NOTTINGHAM
> Watch it, fool. Spotted owls are endangered.

Robin screams in rage and attacks Nottingham, waving the bow like a club. Nottingham bats it aside. They trade blows.

A crossbow bolt ZINGS between them and buries itself in a tree. They break and look at Marian. Robin stumbles down.

> MARIAN
> I said get out.

Nottingham takes a breath, then nods abruptly and mounts. Mrs. Hood starts cackling. Nottingham rides off.

> MRS. HOOD
> You may be my daughter, after all.

Marian throws down the crossbow and stalks away.

EXT. FIELDS - DAY

Nottingham rides along a dirt track. His "S" medallion shines. A sign at a fork points left to

"STAFFORDSHIRE" and right toward "NOTTINGHAMSHIRE." He sighs and goes right.

EXT. FOREST - LATER

Nottingham approaches the edge of a forest. A sign reads, "SHERWOOD FOREST - POPULATION 1." Beside it, two more read, "LITTER ENCOURAGED IF EDIBLE" and "CAUTION - DO NOT FEED THE RANGERS." Nottingham enters.

The path twists, the woods thicken. Suddenly an OLD MAN leaps in front of him. Nottingham's horse shies back.

> OLD MAN
> Beware the haunting. The deep wood sleeps.

Nottingham leans forward and looks at him. The old man looks bewildered a moment, then tries again.

> OLD MAN
> Hunting wakes the damned. Beware the Stag of the Wild Wood.

Nottingham sits back and relaxes.

> NOTTINGHAM
> Stag? Good hunting in here?

> OLD MAN
> No. I mean . . .

The old man gets a crafty expression.

OLD MAN
Depends on what's hunting whom.

Nottingham shakes his head and dismounts. The old man backs away as Nottingham approaches.

OLD MAN
Don't people believe in spirits anymore?

An OWL HOOTS. The old man points.

OLD MAN
See? An evil omen. Begone.

Nottingham stops and looks around. An owl on a nearby branch starts to HOOT again. With a loud SPROING, it keels over and dangles upside down from the branch. A spring sticks out its hind end. The old man jumps up and down.

OLD MAN
Damn cheapskate, imported, low-life . . . .

Nottingham laughs and grabs a skin of wine from his saddle. He sits on a nearby log and offers the old man a drink. After a moment, the old man joins him and grabs the bag.

EXT. FOREST - LATER

Birds SING among the leaves. Butterflies flitter past. Nottingham SLAPS a mosquito. The old man throws down the empty wine skin.

NOTTINGHAM
So, not many deer left?

> OLD MAN
> Damn people breeding like dung-beetles in a cesspit. And always hungry.

> NOTTINGHAM
> That's why they hunt.

> OLD MAN
> That's why they oughta farm smarter. They kill off all the deer, they'll be starving then. May as well starve now and save the deer.

Nottingham looks thoughtful.

> OLD MAN
> If you want to be a good sheriff, start a plague. Haven't had one in years. When I was young we had good plagues.

Nottingham studies the woods.

> NOTTINGHAM
> Noooo. But there's another way to save the deer. This damn job may be good for something, yet.

He fingers his medallion.

EXT. VILLAGE - DAY

Nottingham fingers his medallion, then drops it and finishes tacking up a huge sign beside the door of a tavern. It reads, "NO DEER HUNTING IN SHERWOOD FOREST NATIONAL PARK."

A half dozen SCRAGGLY LOCALS gather to watch.

SCRAGGLE-HAIR
It says . . . deer . . . in . . . forest. Hell, we knew
that.

Nottingham rounds on the fellow.

NOTTINGHAM
It says no hunting in Sherwood.

A YELLOW-TOOTHED PEASANT with a
German accent scratches his head.

YELLOW-TOOTH
Yes, there is. Been there myself.

The other locals nod in confusion. More join them.

SCRAGGLE-HAIR
Pretty good, too. Not as good as it used to be,
mind.

NOTTINGHAM
That's the point. So now it's prohibited.

The CROWD is now over a score. They mutter and
glare.

YELLOW-TOOTH
Pro-what?

SCRAGGLE-HAIR
Means you're in favor.

NOTTINGHAM
Means it's against the law.

The Crowd SNARLS. Fists wave on high.

> PRIM WOMAN
You can't do that.

> NOTTINGHAM
I just did.

Nottingham shoves his way through the near-riot and mounts his horse. The Crowd follows.

> SCRAGGLE-HAIR
Animal lover!

> YELLOW-TOOTH
Alien hater!

Nottingham starts to leave. The prim woman bends near Yellow-Tooth and hisses in his ear.

> PRIM WOMAN
Alien lover. We're the haters.

> YELLOW-TOOTH
Oh. Sorry.
> (beat)
Wait a minute, I'm . . . .

The prim woman waves her fist, ignoring him. Yellow-Tooth backs away. FRIAR TUCK joins the throng.

> SCRAGGLE-HAIR
You cursed tax-collector.

> PRIM WOMAN
Nothing but a common thief.

Nottingham wheels his mount at the edge of town.

NOTTINGHAM
You want lower taxes, you talk King Richard out of his crusade.

TUCK
Sacrilege.

SCRAGGLE-HAIR
He's freeing Jerusalem.

PRIM WOMAN
You'll be damned for that, young man.

Nottingham shakes his head and rides off. Tuck rips down the no hunting sign.

INT. JOHN'S CASTLE STUDY - DAY

John rips a sheet of paper and pitches it. He runs a finger beneath the notes of a musical score and pens a note. Cogsworth walks in and opens his mouth.

JOHN
No. I haven't time to plot.

Cogsworth blinks.

COGSWORTH
Your brother is king, he has no heirs, and it's the twelfth century. It's your duty to conspire, sire.

John scowls and dips his quill in the inkwell.

JOHN
Almost the thirteenth.

Cogsworth shrugs elaborately.

COGSWORTH
That's not why I'm here. One of the sheriffs wishes to complain.

John stops penning notes and looks up.

JOHN
I don't run sheriffs.

COGSWORTH
He says you got him appointed.

John looks confused a second, then nods and tosses down his pen. He follows Cogsworth to the door.

INT. JOHN'S CASTLE HALL

Nottingham paces. Cogsworth enters from a side door and steps aside, looking at the ceiling. John enters the hall.

COGSWORTH
His royal un-majesty, Defender of Ireland . . .

Nottingham whirls and kneels. John ignores Cogsworth and glances from Nottingham's medallion to his face.

JOHN
So you took it. Good.

COGSWORTH
. . . sovereign over no provinces whatsoever . . .

Nottingham stands.

NOTTINGHAM

'Twas not my choice, m'lord. I must protest these taxes I am forced to collect.

JOHN

Protest? Can't say as I blame you.

COGSWORTH

. . . a distant second to the throne of England and scenic points to the south . . .

Nottingham looks surprised.

NOTTINGHAM

But you—

JOHN

Richard's selling land, but he can't raise enough.

COGSWORTH

. . . a grave disappointment to the spirit of his father's acquisitiveness . . .

John turns to Cogsworth.

JOHN

Will you shut up?

Cogsworth looks briefly at John, then back up.

COGSWORTH

. . . Count John.

He scuttles from the room. John sighs.

NOTTINGHAM

Then there's no relief?

John wanders across the room.

>   JOHN
> What could I do? I have nothing to sell.

>   NOTTINGHAM
> If you spoke to—

>   JOHN
> My brother? Or Longchamp?

He snorts. Cogsworth sneaks back in with a tray of
pastries and heads for the dejected Nottingham.

>   NOTTINGHAM
> I don't want the poor going hungry.

>   COGSWORTH
> Torte, m'lord?

Nottingham waves him away, but Cogsworth lingers.

>   JOHN
> Open your eyes, man. They're not hungry.

>   COGSWORTH
> They're not very good tortes. No sugar.

Nottingham stares at John.

>   NOTTINGHAM
> Not . . . but every house—

>   JOHN
> They hide grain, pigs, you name it. You have to
> guess what they've really got.

COGSWORTH
If John were king, we'd have sugar.

Nottingham shakes his head slowly.

NOTTINGHAM
They don't look hungry.

COGSWORTH
Torte reform, that's what we need.

JOHN
Taxes are high, but they're on a par with other countries.

Nottingham hesitates, then nods briefly.

NOTTINGHAM
Then there's the riots. Someone needs to protect foreigners.

COGSWORTH
If John were king, we'd have good torte law.

John rounds on Cogsworth.

JOHN
Would you get out?

Cogsworth scurries away, stuffing a torte in his mouth. John stares after him a moment.

JOHN
I'll speak to Richard again. He's got to stop the riots.

Nottingham bows.

>   NOTTINGHAM
> Thank you, m'lord.

He leaves. John keeps staring at the door Cogsworth went out.

>   JOHN
> Tort law. Curb the barons. Curb the church.

He smiles.

>   JOHN
> Curb the king. I like it.

He looks down and takes a step, then looks back up.

>   JOHN
> I must trick the barons, make them think it's their idea, should I ever be king. Perhaps . . . a "magna carta?"

EXT. DESERT - DAY

CAMELS lumber to a gallop. Curved Arab swords flash in the hands of their white-robed RIDERS.

Two hundred yards away, Richard BELLOWS at a mass of marching SOLDIERS, turning them to face the oncoming horde. Pikes CRASH against each other, CURSES litter the air, and the Arab riders close.

>   RICHARD
> Check.

Suddenly the confusion ends. The soldiers whip their pikes to earth, grounding each against a planted foot, aiming the points at the oncoming camels. Shock ripples across the face of the leading ARAB, then anger.

> RICHARD
> Mate.

A horn SOUNDS. MOUNTED KNIGHTS thunder from between two hills just as the Arab camel-cavalry smashes into the wall of steel. The Arabs falter, two riders thrown amidst the English troops. The Knights crash into the Arab rear, hacking with cavalry sabers.

But the Arabs don't crumble. They throw their camels to the ground for defense, wield swords and short spears, and fight to the last man, taking a heavy toll of English.

Richard glances at his AIDE and dismounts.

> RICHARD
> God, they're good.

He grins, draws his sword, and wades into the fray.

> AIDE
> Your majesty. No.

Richard ignores him, taking on the Arab leader. The Aide hesitates, then follows Richard.

The Arab holds his own, but tires. His last countryman falls. Richard deflects his blade and runs him through. As the Arab collapses, Richard salutes him with his sword.

                    RICHARD
Good show.

                    ARAB
Get a life.

A vulture lands amid the dead.

EXT. FOREST - DAY

Nottingham's Raven flutters to a branch. Nottingham
ducks under a limb and pulls his mount to a stop
before the bird.

                    NOTTINGHAM
I told you to go home.

                    RAVEN
Never. Nikogda.

                    NOTTINGHAM
You don't speak Russian. Who do you think you
are?

                    RAVEN
Po' bird. Po'.

                    NOTTINGHAM
Right. Po. Now look . . .

The bushes rustle fifty yards off and a female DEER
leaps out, followed by a FAWN. An ARROW
THUNKS into a tree ten feet over their heads. They
race off.

Robin bursts from the bushes, bow in hand. He skids
to a halt when he sees Nottingham.

ROBIN

Oops.

NOTTINGHAM

I'll show you "oops," you poacher.

Nottingham spurs his horse. Robin takes off. Nottingham chases Robin down a ravine filled with thorn bushes. Both SWEAR.

EXT. INN - LATER

Robin emerges from the trees near a cheap INN. He skids to a halt, then races inside. Nottingham exits the woods. Robin comes out sipping an ale, sees Nottingham, and takes off.

Nottingham ties his horse and pursues on foot. Marian emerges from the inn and watches.

EXT. RIVER - LATER

Robin stands on a rock beside a river, firing arrow after arrow, missing wildly as Nottingham closes. The Raven dodges and SQUAWKS. Robin drops his bow and charges into a thicket. Nottingham follows.

Nottingham races out of the thicket. Robin chases after. A horde of BEES brings up the rear. Nottingham and Robin jump into the river. The Raven laughs.

The current sweeps Robin and Nottingham along. Nottingham tries to reach Robin. The Raven lands and watches.

>   ROBIN
> You'll never catch me, copper.

>   NOTTINGHAM
> Copper?

>   RAVEN
> Brass.

>   NOTTINGHAM
> You should talk.

Marian appears on the bank.

>   MARIAN
> Robin!

She throws a rope. Robin catches it and she hauls him in, while Nottingham sweeps past. She and Nottingham stare at each other. Robin pants.

>   RAVEN
> Never. More never.

>   MARIAN
> Shut up, Po.

Nottingham and she just stare, until the river curves away.

EXT. VILLAGE - DAY

Nottingham nails a notice on an inn: "WANTED - ROBIN HOOD." A rotund INNKEEPER waddles out to watch.

INNKEEPER
Robin Hood. What you want him for?

NOTTINGHAM
Hunting deer.

INNKEEPER
He can't hunt. I'll do it for you.

Nottingham glares at him. The Innkeeper smiles.

INNKEEPER
Cheaper, too, if I know that welsher.

Nottingham stares a moment longer, then speaks
quietly.

NOTTINGHAM
In Sherwood?

The Innkeeper dries up. He glances back at the sign
and peers at the small print, then swallows and bobs
his head at Nottingham.

INNKEEPER
Get you an ale? On the house?

Nottingham shakes his head.

NOTTINGHAM
I'm looking for Marian, too. She helped him
escape, and neither's been seen for a month.

He mounts.

NOTTINGHAM
And a Friar named Tuck.

He leans down close to the Innkeeper.

> NOTTINGHAM
> He ripped down my signs.

The Innkeeper shudders. Nottingham rides away.

EXT. FOREST CAMP - NIGHT

A roaring fire toasts the carcass of a DEER on a spit. Tuck slowly turns it. Robin fletches an arrow. Marian harangues a small group of MEN, including EDWIN and ROGER.

> MARIAN
> And you, Edwin? What'd you lose?

Robin shakes a finger, a feather glued firmly to it. Tuck bastes the deer with a bucket of melted fat and a stick.

> EDWIN
> Other half o' my farm. Damn inside straight.

Men laugh. Marian glowers. Robin struggles with a feather.

> MARIAN
> I mean, taxes. You, Roger?

Tuck looks at the expanse of unbasted deer, takes a breath, and dips the stick back in the bucket.

> ROGER
> They took my bloody cow.

Marian looks around triumphantly.

MARIAN
See?

Robin flexes his arrow, wedged against his knee, and presses on another feather. His hands are covered with excess feathers.

ROGER
I told them it was a milk cow.

MARIAN
We can't let them ruin the whole country.

Tuck mumbles as fat drips off his stick. The drops flash as they reach the fire. He's still only a tenth done.

ROGER
I mean, you can't get meat from a milk cow.

Robin lifts his fingers. Another feather flutters from his thumb, and the arrow stays bare. He pushes the feather back down, flexing the arrow further.

MARIAN
We must unite. Take back what is ours.

ROGER
Can you?

Tuck glares at the deer. He throws down his stick and lifts the bucket to pour the fat over the deer.

ROBIN
Stick together!

Marian looks gratefully at Robin, then frowns. Robin bends the arrow even more, grimacing at the feathers. The arrow springs free just as Tuck upends the bucket.

The arrow hits Tuck. Tuck YELPS. Fat splashes all over, and a huge FIREBALL erupts. Everyone dives away.

>MARIAN
>Tuck!

>EDWIN
>It's a sign.

>ROBIN
>Oops.

>TUCK
>A sign of bloody ignorance.

Tuck takes off after Robin. Marian gets a gleam in her eye, and rounds on the other men.

>MARIAN
>Yes. A sign. We shall rebel against tyranny, thwart the powers of evil, and recover our lands.

>ROBIN (O.S.)
>Ow. Put that down.

RUSTLING continues as Tuck chases Robin.

>ROGER
>I just want my cow back.

Marian sighs.

ROBIN (O.S.)

Ow!

EXT. FOREST CAMP - DAY

Robin rubs his left arm, bow dangling from his hand. Marian watches an arrow thud into a tree just beyond a huge target.

ROBIN

Ouch.

MARIAN

Better. Rotate your elbow out.

Robin pouts and nocks another arrow. Beyond, Tuck practices quarterstaff against Edwin and Roger. Other Men hack trees with swords, or lunge at bushes with spears. Incompetence reigns supreme.

Marian shakes her head. She yanks up her crossbow and slams a bolt into place. Robin's next arrow hits the target.

ROBIN

There. Did you see that?

MARIAN

Better.

She lifts her crossbow and buries the bolt in the bull's-eye. Robin grits his teeth.

EXT. FOREST - DAY

Robin leads Marian and her BAND of Men down a path to a tiny stream. He starts to cross, then sees the huge JOHN LITTLE on the other side, just starting across. They stare at each other. John Little steps back, sweeping his arm in a gracious bow.

JOHN LITTLE
After you.

Robin hesitates, glances back at the Band, then also steps aside.

ROBIN
No, after you.

The Band spreads out. John Little looks confused.

JOHN LITTLE
You were here first.

He bows again. Robin looks around, then bows deeper.

ROBIN
No, I insist.

JOHN LITTLE
But I am only one. I can wait.

ROBIN
We are so many. You shouldn't have to.

Robin smirks. John Little scowls. Marian steps to the edge of the stream and glares at Robin. Half the Band crosses.

JOHN LITTLE
You mock me.

ROBIN
How could I mock someone so enormous.

Some of the Men laugh.

MARIAN
Robin, let's—

JOHN LITTLE
Brave with your friends, are you.

Robin glowers. He signals and Roger tosses him a quarterstaff.

John Little sets down his pack, pulls out a short tube, and un-telescopes it into a quarterstaff.

JOHN LITTLE
How are you called, quarrelsome one?

ROBIN
I am Robin Hood. And these are my merry men.

MARIAN
What!

TUCK
I am not a merry—

ROBIN
And women.

MARIAN
You presumptuous little—

ROBIN
And your name?

He steps into the stream and John Little matches him.

> JOHN LITTLE
> I hight John Little.

Robin grins and opens his mouth. John Little lifts his staff.

> JOHN LITTLE
> Don't say it.

Robin looks innocent.

> ROBIN
> Say what?

He closes the distance and they click staves.

> ROBIN
> (whisper)
> Little John.

John Little spins his staff and smashes Robin into the stream. Robin gets up, flails for his staff, and falls again.

> JOHN LITTLE
> Now cross.

> ROBIN
> You first.

Robin launches himself at John Little, but slips on a slimy stone and falls. John Little watches. Marian studies the trees.

GRUNTS, SPLASHES, and a few loud THUNKS punctuate the singing of birds.

>ROBIN (O.S.)
>Take that.

A SPLASH. Rocks CLATTER.

>ROBIN (O.S.)
>Well, then, take that.

Another GRUNT and SPLASH. When Marian looks back, Robin is still trying to get his balance. John Little stands, leaning on his staff, looking bored. The Band gapes at Robin. He's soaked.

John Little shakes his head, steps forward, and drags Robin to shore. Marian takes Robin and sets him on a rock.

>ROBIN
>God, he's fast. Never saw him move.

The Band laughs nervously. Marian turns to John Little.

>MARIAN
>Thank you, Mr. Little.

Tuck looks Little up and down, and pokes an arm muscle.

>TUCK
>My, you're the mountain. Ex-soldier?

Marian frowns and fingers her crossbow. John Little moves away from Tuck. Robin gapes at Tuck.

MARIAN
Where lie your loyalties?

The rest of the Band shuffles nervously. Robin gets up.

JOHN LITTLE
Not soldier. Ex-sheriff.

Marian starts to raise her crossbow. John Little twitches his staff; the rest of the Band backs away. Robin goes to Tuck.

JOHN LITTLE
Don't do it, lady. I said, "ex."

MARIAN
Ex?

JOHN LITTLE
Richard's Chancellor fired me when I wouldn't collect his new taxes.

Marian lowers the crossbow. Robin whispers to Tuck.

ROBIN
I didn't know you were of the persuasion.

MARIAN
Nottinghamshire?

John Little nods.

TUCK
What persuasion?

JOHN LITTLE
Took my title, land, everything.

Robin pinches Tuck's arm and smiles suggestively.

ROBIN
I saw you admiring him.

Robin nods toward John Little, and winks at Tuck. Tuck gapes.

MARIAN
Perhaps you could join our band, Mr. Little.

Robin looks over.

ROBIN
Yeah. Show us how you moved so fast, Little John.

John Little scowls and steps toward him. Marian grabs John Little's arm and leans toward Robin, speaking softly.

MARIAN
Knock it off, Cock Robin.

ROBIN
Marian, you promised.

MARIAN
I'll say it louder next time.

John Little smiles. Robin looks from her to Little. Marian steps back and speaks loudly.

             MARIAN
What about it, John Little? We could use a
weapons master.

The rest of the Band MUTTERS agreement. John
Little snorts, then nods, waving a finger at Robin.

             JOHN LITTLE
    As long as he's not your leader.

The Band laughs. Marian slaps John Little's back and
leads the Band away. Robin follows, beside Tuck.

             TUCK
          (whisper)
    "Little John."

Robin snickers. Tuck chuckles.

             ROBIN
    Hey, I crossed the stream first. That means I won,
    right?

Tuck guffaws and throws an arm over Robin's
shoulders.

             TUCK
    History is in the pen of the beholder, my boy.
    And we in the clergy have all the pens.

Robin titters and hugs Tuck, gazing at his eyes.

             ROBIN
    I'm so happy I found out about you.

Tuck rips himself free, brushing his sleeve furiously.

                TUCK
Bugger off. I am not "persuaded."

Robin glances at the others, then back at Tuck.

                ROBIN
I understand.

                TUCK
You!

Tuck hurries forward to catch up with Marian. Robin smiles.

EXT. FOREST CAMP - DAY

John Little drills Roger, Edwin, and others in spear work. Robin practices bow; his string breaks and snaps him in the face.

EXT. FOREST ROAD - DAY

Robin leaps in front of a carriage. It slows, and the DRIVER reaches for a crossbow. Robin draws and fires. The Driver gapes at the size of the miss, then raises his crossbow.

A THUNK, and the crossbow flies from his hand. He looks to the side and Marian smiles, leaning her own crossbow against her shoulder. The Driver's eyes skip over her and back to Robin, who pumps his fist in victory and waves his bow.

The Driver gapes at Robin. Marian smolders. The rest of the Band appears, wielding spears.

EXT. FOREST CAMP - DAY

Marian's Band dumps two small bags of coins on the ground. Marian chases them back to practice. She watches John Little demonstrate sword grips, then whacks Robin's bow arm with a stick and points at his footing.

EXT. FOREST ROAD - DAY

Tuck leaps in front of a carriage, but falls down. Marian and John Little smash into the horses, driving them aside.

The driver reaches for a crossbow; an arrow ZINGS in front of his eyes. He drops the crossbow. Marian raises an eyebrow at Robin. Robin looks at his bow, then grins.

EXT. FOREST CAMP - DAY

The Band ogles a table filled with small chests, pouches, loose jewelry. Marian chases them back to practice.

EXT. WOODS - DAY

King Richard and a small ESCORT ride along a hilly trail. As they pass beneath trees, a NET falls over them. Fifty leather-clad WARRIORS pull the net tight and stab all the Escort.

> RICHARD
> Foul devils. Let me out. Fight like men.

Richard keeps struggling and SWEARING as the Warriors cut off the extra net and hold him with the remainder. They drag him before the helmeted COUNT WEIMAR, who speaks with a thick German accent.

> RICHARD
>
> Count Weimar. You have outdone yourself.

> WEIMAR
>
> Hello, Richard. Feel up to a ransom? I was thinking 97,000 pounds.

Richard struggles again, vainly.

> RICHARD
>
> You'll not get a cent over forty-three. Such unbrave deeds shall not be rewarded.

> WEIMAR
>
> 89,000, then. You're a hero, after all.

> RICHARD
>
> Fifty-one. My coffers are bare, after my great success.

Richard stops struggling and Weimar hands him a flask. Richard drinks through the netting.

> WEIMAR
>
> You finally took Jerusalem? That's worth something. Seventy-eight.

> RICHARD
>
> Not the city. But I still won. Fifty-seven.

> WEIMAR
>
> Seventy-three. I've got horrible alimony.

Richard chokes and throws the flask on the ground.

> RICHARD
> We're already over the greatest ransom in history. Sixty-two.

Weimar leans close and glares. Richard glares back.

> WEIMAR
> Sixty-eight.

> RICHARD
> Sixty-five.

> WEIMAR
> Sixty-six.

> RICHARD
> Done.

They lean back and smile. A CLERK runs up with a small desk and unrolls a parchment. He holds quills. Weimar and Richard sign.

> WEIMAR
> I'd have gone to fifty-seven, you know.

> RICHARD
> I'd have gone seventy-four. And 'twas still an ugly deed.

Weimar shrugs.

> WEIMAR
> I ain't no pretty woman.

EXT. NOTTINGHAM'S ESTATE - DAY

Nottingham chases his animals to their cages.

> NOTTINGHAM
> Playtime's over. Shoo. Back.

They all go home, except the Raven sits on the roof and preens itself.

> NOTTINGHAM
> You, too.

> RAVEN
> More never.

A MESSENGER gallops up, all asweat. He dismounts as his HORSE pants, tongue hanging down. The Messenger looks at his mount.

> MESSENGER
> Horses don't pant.

The Horse sucks in its tongue and snorts. The Messenger hands a scroll to Nottingham.

> NOTTINGHAM
> The seal's broken.

> MESSENGER
> You try riding twenty miles with a scroll in your hand.

> NOTTINGHAM
> The ink's all run.

> MESSENGER
> I was sweating. Had to wipe my head with something.

> NOTTINGHAM
> I can't read a word.

> MESSENGER
> Count John wants you. There's been another raid in Sherwood.

Nottingham scowls at him.

> MESSENGER
> Well, shit, the seal was broke.

Nottingham grabs his own horse and gallops off.

> MESSENGER
> Blimey, no pleasing some people.

EXT. JOHN'S CASTLE YARD - LATER

Nottingham rides into the forecourt, tosses the reins to a STABLEMAN, and races in the main entrance.

INT. JOHN'S CASTLE HALL

John paces. Nottingham enters. John throws his goblet against the wall.

> JOHN
> Richard's been taken.

Nottingham hesitates. Cogsworth rushes in, brushing straw from his clothes.

NOTTINGHAM
Arabs?

John waves dismissively. Cogsworth sees the goblet and dashes over to clean up the mess.

JOHN
Germans.

Nottingham gapes. Cogsworth looks up, then runs out.

JOHN
Don't ask me why he took a shortcut. Now there's ransom.

Cogsworth runs back in with a tuppence.

JOHN
66,000 pounds.

Cogsworth drops his hand.

COGSWORTH
My lord. Congratulations.

John whirls, incensed.

NOTTINGHAM
He may be right, my lord.

Nottingham bows. Cogsworth grins.

NOTTINGHAM
That's like a hundred billion pounds, eight hundred years from now. There's no way to raise that much.

>   JOHN
> I am not king yet, nor likely to be. Longchamp
> has tripled taxes.

Cogsworth looks at his tuppence, and stuffs it in a
pocket. Nottingham shakes his head.

>   NOTTINGHAM
> They're already—

>   JOHN
> And you're so far behind he's talking treason.

Cogsworth inches back, then sneaks from the hall.

>   JOHN
> And accusing me, for recommending you.

>   NOTTINGHAM
> I've been busy.

>   JOHN
> I know. Robin Hood.

He gestures and stalks outside. Nottingham follows.

EXT. JOHN'S CASTLE YARD

A fat, balding EXECUTIONER sits on the edge of a
scaffold, twiddling his thumbs, swinging his heels.
He's all alone. He scratches an ear through his black
cowl, heaves a sigh, and stands. He reaches both
hands before him, takes a step, and trips over a
headsman's axe.

Nottingham blinks in surprise.

John snaps his fingers and points at a score of mounted Guards.

            JOHN
    They're yours. Use them.

Nottingham frowns, then mounts. John grabs his bridle, whispering for his ears alone.

            JOHN
    It'll do the peasants no good if Longchamp replaces you. You're fairer than most.

Nottingham looks down, then back at John. A tiny half-smile flickers and disappears.

            NOTTINGHAM
    Thank you, m'lord.

Behind a wagon, Cogsworth watches Nottingham ride off with his new Guards.

EXT. FOREST - DAY

Marian, Robin, Tuck, and the others hide in the brush. A rich carriage approaches. Marian raises her arm.

Cogsworth suddenly rides in from the opposite direction. He cuts into the brush.

            COGSWORTH
    Marian?

John Little yanks him down and covers his mouth. Tuck pulls the horse into the trees. Marian and Robin sneak up.

ROBIN
I'm Robin Hood. Who are you?

Marian shushes him. She signals John Little; he lets Cogsworth go. Cogsworth pulls out a small notebook and flips it open.

MARIAN
What do you have?

COGSWORTH
Nottingham's got guards. It's a trap.

Marian and John Little glance back at the path. The fancy carriage passes their spot.

JOHN LITTLE
If this is a trick, you little sponge . . .

MARIAN
Leave him be. Better safe than swinging.

Robin's eyes go big. His hand clutches his throat.

ROBIN
On a rope?

John Little rolls his eyes.

JOHN LITTLE
What did you think they'd do with thieves?

Hooves sound in the distance. Marian and John Little creep up near the path. Robin fingers his neck.

ROBIN
I don't know.

Nottingham and a score of armored, heavily-armed Guards thunder past, following the carriage. Robin shudders.

> ROBIN
> Lock us up. Probation in a year or two. Time off for good behavior.

Tuck slaps him on the back. Robin SQUEAKS and jumps a foot.

> TUCK
> Don't sweat it. They won't take us alive.

The horses recede.

> ROBIN
> Uh. Thanks.

> TUCK
> Glad to help.

Robin swallows.

EXT. FARM HOUSE - DAY

A COCK CROWS on the roof. The Raven lands and tries to OUT-CROW it. Nottingham and his Guards loom out of the fog with a wagon.

A rotund FAMILY scurries away. A half dozen Guards round them up while the rest fan out and rifle the house, barn, and countryside. Nottingham sits on his horse and watches.

One Guard comes out of the house with a bolt of rich cloth. Another digs in the hollow of a tree and removes a bag of silver coins. A third rolls a cask from the barn, and two more bring bushels of potatoes.

EXT. FARM HOUSE - LATER

A table in front of the house is heaped with bushels of apples, loaves of bread, two hams, and everything else the Guards have found. A Guard tosses two new axe-heads on top.

The family stares at the pile. Nottingham gets off his horse and lifts an axe head.

> NOTTINGHAM
> Good steel.

He looks at the father.

> NOTTINGHAM
> Starving, wasn't it? Last visit?

The FATHER shudders. The MOTHER wails and clutches him. A SON glares, and a DAUGHTER winks at Nottingham when she thinks no one is watching. Nottingham tosses down the axe head.

> NOTTINGHAM
> People have been hanged for less.

The family stares at their wealth. Nottingham signals SERGEANT PORKERS. Porkers and a couple of other Guards count the coins and take a third, take a third of everything else, and load it onto Nottingham's wagon.

One Guard meticulously cuts each apple into thirds, tossing one piece of each in the wagon. Nottingham slaps him up the side of the head and makes him divide whole bushels into three piles.

As Nottingham turns back, another Guard tosses one axe head into the wagon. Porkers picks up the bolt of cloth and levels his sword over it.

> NOTTINGHAM
> Leave it.

> PORKERS
> Sir?

> NOTTINGHAM
> Call it an axe head. We've got our third.

> PORKERS
> But we're to take—

> NOTTINGHAM
> I said leave it.

Porkers drops the cloth like it bit him. Nottingham and all the Guards mount. Nottingham looks back at the family.

> NOTTINGHAM
> Richard's tax is a fourth when you haven't tried to cheat. Think about it.

They ride off. The family yells after them.

> FATHER
> Cursed French.

MOTHER
Richard, my ass. You sheriffs are thieves.

SON
You'll pay for this.

DAUGHTER
Cute, wasn't he?

The Mother grabs her by the ear and drags her in the house. The Father looks at his Son and waves at the table.

FATHER
Hide all this.

INT. HUT - DAY

Marian waves at a mass of treasure on a table. The rest of the Band mills around, bumping into makeshift furniture.

MARIAN
What are we supposed to do with this?

John Little scratches his head.

ROBIN
Spend it.

TUCK
We're rich, Marian.

MARIAN
And what good will it do us?

John Little looks thoughtful. Tuck rubs his chin and frowns.

> ROBIN
> What good? Horses. Carriages. Grand manors. Servants. We'll be nobles.

> MARIAN
> And who will sell us these things. What story do we tell, that we came by this?

> ROBIN
> Inheritance. No, we're immigrants. No . . .

> MARIAN
> Immigrants, perhaps. To Ireland, or France.

> JOHN LITTLE
> I have no wish to abandon my country.

Marian looks from him to Tuck. Tuck sighs and glances up.

> TUCK
> Forgive me, lord. Moment of weakness.

He looks at Marian.

> TUCK
> I'll take it to the Bishop. He's always looking to expand the seminary.

Marian shakes her head.

> MARIAN
> The church is rich enough. Why are we out here?

The three men glance at each other.

>   ROBIN
> Upward mobility?

>   TUCK
> Attune with nature?

>   JOHN LITTLE
> Savor my cooking?

Tuck and Robin gag. Marian slaps Robin on the side of the head.

>   MARIAN
> Taxes, you dolts.

The others nod agreement. Robin rubs his head. Tuck and John Little move back.

>   MARIAN
> And if the problem is taxes, what do we do with all this?

John Little looks at the pile. Tuck looks at John Little.

>   TUCK
> Give it to Nottingham?

He ducks. John Little looks down at him, betrayed.

>   MARIAN
> You're getting close.

Tuck stands up.

                    TUCK
          Really?

John Little flicks him in the side of the head.

                    JOHN LITTLE
          We give it to the taxed.

Marian closes her eyes and slowly opens them.

                    MARIAN
          What a startling idea.

                    ROBIN
          But Marian—

She tosses a sack of coins at Robin.

                    MARIAN
          Fine. You don't have to. Disguise yourself, go to
          town, and have fun.

Robin grins.

                    ROBIN
          Really?

He suddenly looks thoughtful and dashes to the door.

                    ROBIN
          I mean, thanks.

He races off. John Little looks from the door to
Marian.

                    JOHN LITTLE
          But you said . . .

Tuck chuckles.

> TUCK
> You ever seen him gamble?

INT. TAVERN - NIGHT

Smoke and song fill a rough tavern. Robin, thinly disguised in a scraggly beard and beret, tosses dice on the floor. A FAT BARMAID shrieks laughter as four MEN scoop up their winnings. Robin shakes his head and sets out more coins.

EXT. FOREST ROAD - DAY

Nottingham and Guards gallop up to a WELL-DRESSED MERCHANT, standing by an empty wagon and shaking his fist at the distance. Nottingham purses his lips and takes off after the thieves.

INT. TAVERN - NIGHT

Robin sits in the tavern, drinking and tossing dice. He pulls off his fake beard and scratches his chin. The Fat Barmaid stares at him a moment; her eyes go big.

EXT. FOREST CLEARING - DAY

Marian and John Little ride up to a small hut. A filthy CRONE comes out and peers up at them. Marian gets down and hands her a silver pitcher. The Crone gapes.

EXT. FOREST ROAD - DAY

Robin and Tuck, with half the Band, stop a lone Jewish MERCHANT atop a wagon covered with a cloth tarp.

> ROBIN
> What's in the wagon, alien?

The merchant moves his mouth a couple of times.

> TUCK
> Speak up, infidel.

The merchant flutters his hands.

> MERCHANT
> They're just babies. Please don't hurt them.

Robin covers him with a wavering bow. Tuck rides over and yanks the tarp off the wagon. It's full of cages, filled with PUPPIES, KITTENS, BUNNIES, and CANARIES. They set up a DIN.

> ROBIN
> All right!

The Band looks confused. Robin grins.

EXT. FOREST CAMP - LATER

Robin grins as he, Tuck, and half the Band ride up. Edwin drives the merchant's tarp-covered wagon.

Marian and John Little come over. Tuck rips off the cover.

MARIAN
Why ever did you . . . .

Robin grins. He and Tuck dismount.

ROBIN
They're foreign. I figure we can eat the—

Marian backhands him. He smashes into a tree ten feet away.

TUCK
Actually, we could naturalize them. Make them all English . . . .

He cowers from Marian. She signs to John Little, and they climb onto the wagon, shoving Edwin to the ground.

EXT. FOREST - LATER

Nottingham and his Guards wheel their horses beside the Jewish merchant, who sits beside the trail, slumped against a log. The Guards sag in their saddles, panting.

NOTTINGHAM
They took your what?

MERCHANT
They said it was King's policy.

Nottingham turns purple. The merchant looks down the path, shaking his head.

MERCHANT
Just babies.

NOTTINGHAM
They've gone too far.

He spurs his horse to a gallop.

EXT. POOR VILLAGE

Marian and John Little pass out caged animals to CHILDREN, who SCREAM in delight. ADULTS come out. Marian gives each a few coins.

MARIAN
To help care for them.

The people look at their children, at the coins, at Marian. A WEATHERED WOMAN grabs Marian's arm.

WEATHERED WOMAN
Bless you, Marian.

Marian blinks in surprise.

MARIAN
You know me?

The Weathered Woman smiles.

WEATHERED WOMAN
Robin and Marian. And your band. You're getting famous, child.

Marian quivers. She grabs John Little and rushes him away.

EXT. FOREST CAMP - LATER

Tuck blocks Roger's quarterstaff and holds up his hand. Edwin leans on his wooden practice sword and looks over. The rest of the Band catches the mood and gets quiet.

TUCK
Horses. Coming fast.

Robin looks over from the archery target.

ROBIN
That's just—

TUCK
Not like this.

Roger and Edwin exchange a glance. Suddenly everyone races off, a few with horses but most on foot.

Nottingham and ten exhausted Guards burst into the clearing, swords drawn.

NOTTINGHAM
Burn it.

The Guards scurry around, destroying the archery target, setting fire to tents and the crude hut. Nottingham slowly circles the area, leaning down from his horse. Porkers trails him.

PORKERS
Tracks everywhere.

Nottingham stops and points at wagon ruts.

NOTTINGHAM
This way.

He charges off. Porkers wearily waves at the troops and follows. Only two of the Guards come after.

EXT. FIELD - LATER

Nottingham trudges along, leading his horse. Porkers staggers beside him, the only Guard left. Nottingham points at the ground and changes direction slightly.

EXT. POOR VILLAGE - LATER

Nottingham rides up at a walk, alone. He glances at the ground, then back at the village. He frowns.

In the village, children roll on the ground, laughing and playing with a mass of puppies, kittens, and bunnies. CHIRPING floods the air, along with YIPS and SQUEALS.

Nottingham dismounts and walks toward the village. He stops, snatches off his "S" medallion and fancy cap, and hides them in a saddlebag. He continues into the midst of the villagers.

The Weathered Woman waves at him from a bench.

WEATHERED WOMAN
Welcome, stranger. We've been visited by an angel.

NOTTINGHAM
Ma'am?

WEATHERED WOMAN
Marian, good sir. Surely you've heard of Robin
Hood and Marian.

She gets up and waddles beside him, pointing toward
an inn.

INT. COMMON ROOM OF INN - NIGHT

Nottingham sits in shock. The Weathered Woman
still regales him. A couple of other PATRONS nurse
drinks and play with a kitten. Another Patron talks to
a canary in a cage.

WEATHERED WOMAN
I tell you, they'll make songs about that pair. Rob
from the rich, and give to us poor folks, they do.

Nottingham shakes his head.

WEATHERED WOMAN
A master of archery and disguise, our Robin.

NOTTINGHAM
(mumbling)
Must be someone else.

WEATHERED WOMAN
It's so romantic. I hope they get married. Never
did, myself, but it'd make a better story, don't you
think?

NOTTINGHAM
Hmmm? What?

His eyes widen and he turns to her.

                    NOTTINGHAM
Hope they what?

                    WEATHERED WOMAN
Get married.
    (sigh)
Robin and Marian. Got a ring, you know?

She laughs. Nottingham gapes.

                    NOTTINGHAM
She's his sister, you dotty hag!

The Weathered Woman snorts.

                    WEATHERED WOMAN
Nonsense. They work together too well to be
related.

Nottingham stares, then stumbles out into the night.

EXT. NOTTINGHAM'S ESTATE - DAY

Nottingham pumps a well. The water gushes into an
intricate trough system that runs alongside all the
cages, filling half-barrels, buckets, or cups inside each
cage.

Longchamp's carriage rolls up and his Guards sit at
attention, except for the Coarse Guard who races
over to the pygmy hippo pen. He pulls out a fork and
gazes inside.

                    COARSE GUARD
My exquisite entree. Someday we'll be together.

The pygmy hippo FARTS in his face. The other Guards laugh. Longchamp alights and signals the Coarse Guard back in line.

Nottingham stops pumping and rubs his hands on his trousers. Longchamp leads him a few paces aside and waves at the zoo.

>LONGCHAMP
>Still like animals?

>NOTTINGHAM
>I'm getting your taxes.

>LONGCHAMP
>Behind. But other issue.

The Coarse Guard sneaks back toward the pygmy hippo again.

>LONGCHAMP
>You blame Richard.

>NOTTINGHAM
>It's his bloody—

>LONGCHAMP
>No!

The Coarse Guard freezes, one foot on the fence.

>LONGCHAMP
>Richard hero. Church honors. Glory of English.

The Coarse Guard resumes climbing into the pygmy hippo pen.

NOTTINGHAM
He's never in England. And he's robbing them
blind. I don't—

LONGCHAMP
Said no.

The Coarse Guard jumps and glances at Longchamp,
who's not looking at him. The Coarse Guard
swallows and climbs back out.

LONGCHAMP
Not demean Richard. Sheriffs villains.

Nottingham glares at him. Longchamp leans closer.

LONGCHAMP
Truth treason. Comprehend?

Nottingham's jaw works vainly. Longchamp starts to
turn away. The Coarse Guard tiptoes into position.
The other Guards smirk.

LONGCHAMP
Punish peasants. Skim off top. Else traitor.

He glances back. Nottingham glares. Longchamp
smiles and returns to his Guards. He scans them, then
looks away.

LONGCHAMP
Keep eye on you.

The Coarse Guard cringes. Nottingham fumes as
Longchamp gets into his carriage and rolls away.

INT. JOHN'S CASTLE HALL - DAY

Cogsworth ushers in the Blue-, Red-, and Green-clad barons. John watches them approach.

> BLUE BARON
> You cannot pay this absurd ransom.

> RED BARON
> It's ruining us.

> GREEN BARON
> I had to fire one mistress.

The Blue Baron shoves the Green Baron to the rear.

> RED BARON
> Have you no ambition, Count John?

John holds up a hand, and the barons pause.

> JOHN
> It was never in my hands. You know Longchamp oversees Richard's interests.

The Blue Baron sputters.

> BLUE BARON
> But you've got support.

> RED BARON
> The populace hates the taxes.

> GREEN BARON
> 'Course, they still love Richard.

Blue and Red grab Green and shove him toward the door. Cogsworth opens it so they can toss Green out.

Longchamp stands in the open doorway. He raises an eyebrow. Blue and Red release Green, and the three scramble to the side, bowing. Longchamp enters.

> LONGCHAMP
> My, my, my, my, my. What A Mess.

He looks from the Barons to John.

> LONGCHAMP
> Someone fugitive?

John just looks at the barons.

> JOHN
> I trust you won't return?

The barons look from him to Longchamp. They scurry out the door. John waves to a chair, and sinks into one himself.

> JOHN
> Good timing, Longchamp.

Longchamp looks over his shoulder as Cogsworth shuts the door.

> LONGCHAMP
> *I* think so.

He frowns at John a moment, then waves Cogsworth to leave and paces across the room, ignoring the chairs.

> LONGCHAMP
Don't like your sheriff.

> JOHN
Nottingham?

Cogsworth returns with a tray and two goblets of wine. Longchamp glares, but John takes a glass. Longchamp hesitates, then takes the other. Cogsworth sets down the tray and stands by the wall.

> LONGCHAMP
Not hanging delinquent taxpayers. Not one.

John purses his lips.

> JOHN
He's about caught up, though, I thought.

Cogsworth pulls out a tiny notebook and jots something down.

> LONGCHAMP
Not right. Sheriff's take heat. Richard spotless.

> JOHN
I'd think Richard more concerned about getting away from the Germans.

Longchamp flutters a hand, then whips his eyes toward Cogsworth. Cogsworth jerks the notebook out of sight and looks innocent.

> LONGCHAMP
Almost enough for that.

He looks back at John. Cogsworth sneaks out his notebook.

> LONGCHAMP
> Your friend. Straighten him. And clear out Robin Hood. Sick of them.

Cogsworth stops scribbling, stuffs the notebook in his pocket, and darts to open the door one step ahead of Longchamp. John looks thoughtful.

> JOHN
> Robin Hood.

He chews his lip.

INT. BROTHEL - DAY

A MADAM stands stiff and furious. CRAFTSMEN and LOWER NOBLES mingle to the rear, blocked by Nottingham's Guards. A CURLY-HAIRED Guard looks over Nottingham's shoulder.

Nottingham watches a ONE-EYED Guard and another Guard search each of several satin-clad GIRLS in the front of the room.

> CURLY-HAIR
> My turn yet?

A BRUNETTE waves at him.

> NOTTINGHAM
> Pay attention.

The Brunette grabs One-Eye's hand and slips it down her bodice.

                    BRUNETTE
You didn't check here, yet.

                    MADAM
Don't do that. Not for free.

A half-dozen Guards, including Porkers, CLATTER
down the stairs, arms laden with jewelry. Nottingham
points to a table. They divide the loot and take a third
outside.

                    MADAM
You can't do this.

The two Guards finish with the brunette and turn
toward Nottingham. He gestures to a REDHEAD
leaning in the corner.

                    NOTTINGHAM
You missed her.

                    REDHEAD
I was hoping you'd do me yourself.

Nottingham looks away. One-Eye puts out his hands.
The Redhead sulks and raises her arms for his search.

                    MADAM
You already taxed them.

She points at the craftsmen and nobles.

                    MADAM
Taxing me is double . . . something.

                    PORKERS
M'lord, look.

Nottingham turns back to the Redhead. One-Eye crawls from beneath her voluminous skirt, holding a huge diamond.

ONE-EYE
You'll never believe where this was.

The madam spins toward the Redhead, glaring daggers.

MADAM
What did you tell him, you . . . ?

The Redhead smiles and gestures at Nottingham.

REDHEAD
His men are so thorough.

Nottingham looks from her to the madam. He steps to the Redhead and takes the diamond from the Guard. He hefts it.

NOTTINGHAM
Our orders say to hang the more serious cheaters.

He stares at the madam. She flinches.

NOTTINGHAM
Might this be yours?

MADAM
No! Not at all. What would I do with such a thing?

Nottingham bounces the gem on his palm. He glances at the Redhead, who beams at the madam.

NOTTINGHAM
Is it yours?

REDHEAD
Looks to me like it's yours.

MADAM
I'll ki—

Nottingham glances at the Madam. She struggles to maintain her composure.

MADAM
Kick myself, for not knowing.

Nottingham looks at the Redhead.

NOTTINGHAM
I think you'll have to come with us.

REDHEAD
I was so hoping you'd ask.

She weaves her body at him, lifts his hand to her lips, then slides his fingers down the side of her throat. He shudders and snatches his hand away.

NOTTINGHAM
Such a lovely neck, to grace a mournful noose.

She gasps. The madam smirks; the Redhead points at her.

REDHEAD
She—

MADAM
We accept your justice.

The Redhead gives the madam a rude Italian gesture.

MADAM
If you are through, I bid you good day.

Nottingham points to the Redhead. Guards grab her.

REDHEAD
No! It was her—

One-Eye clasps a hand over her mouth.

PORKERS
Shall I get a rope, sir?

The Redhead starts kicking. The madam looks scandalized.

MADAM
Not here. You'll ruin the ambience.

Nottingham looks around and raises an eyebrow.

NOTTINGHAM
Not a swinging place, is it?

The Redhead bites One-Eye's hand. He yanks it back and YELPS. Nottingham signals. The Guards drag the Redhead toward the door.

REDHEAD
(to Madam)
You witch. You'll freeze in hell for this.

NOTTINGHAM
Freeze?

REDHEAD
In your next life, you'll be French.

NOTTINGHAM
Freeze?

The Redhead looks at him as she disappears through the door.

REDHEAD
Dante's "Inferno," you imbecile.

Nottingham shakes his head and follows her out.

NOTTINGHAM
Not written yet.

EXT. WOODS - DAY

A bald, desiccated, blackened CORPSE dangles from the limb of a tree in the falling dusk. Nottingham halts his Guards and rides back to look at the Redhead tied in the back of his tax wagon.

REDHEAD
You have got to be the most unimaginative man in England.

He climbs into the wagon.

REDHEAD
All the things you could do with my body, and you're going to hang me.

He pulls a knife and cuts her bonds.

> NOTTINGHAM
> Strip.

She slowly smiles.

> CURLY-HAIR
> Do I get a turn?

Porkers backhands him. Curly-Hair tumbles to the ground.

> NOTTINGHAM
> Thank you, sergeant.

Porkers nods. Nottingham roots through the tax loot and pulls out a rough woolen dress. He throws it at the girl.

> NOTTINGHAM
> I said strip. And put that on.

She wrinkles her nose at the wool and fluffs her skirt.

EXT. WOODS - LATER

The satin skirt swirls in the breeze. The desiccated corpse dangles from a limb, bedecked in the Redhead's clothes. Porkers stands in his stirrups and pats locks of red hair on the skull. He pulls a sticky strand off his fingers.

The Redhead sits atop Nottingham's wagon, her hair decidedly shorter. She grabs the reins from the driver and steers up beside Nottingham. She bats her eyes. He rides off.

EXT. SHORE - NIGHT

Nottingham beats on the door of a hut. A bleary-eyed FISHERMAN opens it. His FRIZZY WIFE peers from behind.

> NOTTINGHAM
> I need a passage to Ireland.

> FISHERMAN
> I ain't going there. Bunch of—

> FRIZZY WIFE
> Let's see your metal.

She shoves her husband aside and looks at the gold Nottingham shakes out into her hand.

> FRIZZY WIFE
> How many?

> NOTTINGHAM
> One.

He reaches beside the door and pulls out the furious Redhead. He grabs her chin and makes her look at him.

> NOTTINGHAM
> You never come back to England. Right?

The Redhead lets out a breath, then nods. He lets go.

> REDHEAD
> Why Ireland, for Christ's sake?

The corner of his mouth twitches.

                    NOTTINGHAM
Count John says there aren't enough redheads. Be
fruitful and multiply.

She stares a second, then laughs. He tosses her a small
pouch, turns away, and takes two steps.

She grabs him, spins him around, and busses him
severely. He breaks away, and she saunters back to
the hut.

                    NOTTINGHAM
Why'd you do that?

She spins, tilting her head saucily.

                    REDHEAD
You deserved it. I just wonder who you're saving
yourself for.

She laughs at his expression.

INT. TAVERN - NIGHT

A serving WENCH laughs. Robin rolls the dice on
the floor. He groans. Five men chuckle, clap him on
the back, and scoop up money.

The Wench leans on the bar beside a tray of dirty
mugs. The Fat Barmaid slaps down a rag and blows
hair out of her eyes.

                    FAT BARMAID
That's so nice of Robin Hood.

                    WENCH
What, losing?

The Fat Barmaid nods, studying him. The Innkeeper stalks toward them; they both grab mugs and start furiously wiping.

FAT BARMAID
Robbing the wealthy and aiding the poor. This is so much better than handouts.

The Wench wrinkles her brow.

FAT BARMAID
Lets the men keep their self-respect.

The Wench rolls her eyes.

A FARMER races in. He skids to a stop, looks around, and scuttles over to the dice game.

FARMER
Nottingham's coming.

Robin leaps up. He dashes toward the back. The Innkeeper intercepts him and hides him under the bar.

Nottingham enters. Conversation lags, then surges as everyone forces a laugh, eyes flitting now and then to Nottingham.

Nottingham frowns. The Innkeeper saunters up.

INNKEEPER
I paid my tax.

NOTTINGHAM
Richard has been freed. He thanks you for his ransom. Pass the word.

Subdued CHEERING ripples through the room. Some PATRONS openly stare at Nottingham.

                    INNKEEPER
He paid for that with estates in France.

The Wench walks by with a tray of mugs. She looks Nottingham up and down.

                    WENCH
We know where taxes go.

A STOUT FELLOW raises his glass. Everyone in the room now watches Nottingham.

                    STOUT FELLOW
You damned sorcerer.

Nottingham stalks over and hauls Stout Fellow to his feet.

                    NOTTINGHAM
What are you talking about?

Stout Fellow quails, but takes heart at SHOUTS of encouragement.

                    STOUT FELLOW
We heard about that girl you hung. Turned black and wrinkly inside a day.

                    FAT BARMAID
'Tain't natural.

                    STOUT FELLOW
Foul witchcraft.

Nottingham glares, then tosses him to the floor.

> NOTTINGHAM
> The estates in France were taken by Philip while Richard was held in Germany. Richard means to recover them.

CRIES of disbelief greet the announcement. Then delight.

> INNKEEPER
> Brave Richard.

> WENCH
> Cursed French.

> FAT BARMAID
> He'll get them back.

Nottingham shakes his head.

> NOTTINGHAM
> Even though he "sold" them?

No one hears him. The Innkeeper signals the two barmaids.

> INNKEEPER
> Drinks on the house.

> STOUT FELLOW
> Long live Richard.

> FAT BARMAID
> And Robin Hood.

The room goes still. Nottingham turns to the barmaid.

> FAT BARMAID
> I mean . . . he likes . . . lower taxes . . . .

Nottingham stares as she trails off.

> NOTTINGHAM
> Speaking of which, they're up to fifty percent. For Richard's new armies.

CRIES of outrage follow, as he spins and stalks out. A mug SMASHES into the door behind him.

> STOUT FELLOW
> Way to go, Greta.

The Fat Barmaid covers her mouth, looking horrified. Behind the bar, Robin slowly stands.

EXT. FOREST - DAY

Nottingham glances at his full tax wagon, then the sun. He signals Porkers.

> NOTTINGHAM
> Take this to Longchamp. I'm going to try the Abbey again.

Porkers scratches his head.

> PORKERS
> Don't you get tired of them?

NOTTINGHAM
No choice. John says the church should pay tax on their business.

PORKERS
But they never—

NOTTINGHAM
I said I'd try.

Porkers shrugs. He waves half the troop toward Nottingham. No one goes. He waves again.

ONE-EYE
Not my turn.

CURLY-HAIR
I'm sick of wine.

Other Guards MUTTER agreement.

PORKERS
Shut up. You, you . . . .

He fingers ten of the Guards to go with Nottingham, including Curly-Hair. Porkers salutes and leads his own group off with the wagon. Nottingham rides cross-country.

EXT. FOREST - LATER

Roger sits in a tree, staring down a trail. Sergeant Porkers appears around a bend. The wagon follows.

Roger looks back and cups his hands around his mouth.

ROGER
(words; not a "sound")
Bird call. Bird call.

Edwin looks up from fifty feet away, then yells back to the rest of Robin and Marian's Band.

EDWIN
(words)
Bird call.

The Band leaps up. Marian rolls her eyes. They get into ambush positions along the trail. Edwin climbs a tree beside Roger. Half-barrels hang upright on ropes from several limbs.

EXT. ABBEY

Nottingham sits his horse in front of the main abbey gate. His Guards inch away until he scowls at them.

NOTTINGHAM
Our Lady of Blithe Spirits. Ahoy.

A NUN appears atop the outer wall, above the door.

NUN
"Ab. Bee." Abbey. We are not a ship.

NOTTINGHAM
Does that mean I don't get the wave-off? You'll pay the tax?

The MOTHER SUPERIOR appears beside the nun.

NUN
You're all wet.

MOTHER SUPERIOR
You know the Bishop won't allow it.

NOTTINGHAM
You own vast tracts of land. You sell goods like any peddler. In all fairness, Count John—

The nuns up-end a cask of wine on the wall. It SPLASHES all over Nottingham and Curly-Hair.

EXT. FOREST

A mass of water SMASHES onto Porkers and his Guards, knocking them all to the ground.

In the trees above, Roger and Edwin wave short swords and laugh. Half-barrels dangle from tree limbs, dripping.

Robin and Marian step into the path. Porkers grabs a stirrup and struggles to his feet. Tuck, John Little, and the rest of the Band leap from the bushes and bind the other Guards.

Porkers is the only threat. He draws his sword. Robin and Marian fire, and the sword flies from Porkers's hand. He looks at the nick partway down one finger.

PORKERS
Watch it, Robin.

Robin smiles and looks cocky. Marian glares and cocks her crossbow.

In the tree above Porkers, Roger yanks an arrow from a branch beside his head, and glares at Robin.

                    ROBIN
         Sorry.

Marian slaps in another bolt and hefts her crossbow.

                    MARIAN
         Tell Nottingham I heard about his redhead.

Porkers starts to grin.

                    PORKERS
         Really? We—

Her bolt SLAMS into his pommel, half an inch from
his hand.

                    MARIAN
         I expect a little hanging now and then. Some
         burning, maybe. But sorcery goes too far.

She looks around. The Band departs with most of the
goods from the tax wagon. She steps back.

                    MARIAN
         Tell him the wedding is off.

She grabs Robin's shoulder and they dash away.

                    PORKERS
         Wedding?

Porkers shakes his head and turns toward his bound
troops.

EXT. ABBEY

Nottingham wheels his mount. His Guards close in as he leaves.

          NUN
That's all you'll ever get.

          MOTHER SUPERIOR
Tell Count John our allegiance is to God.

Nottingham licks his lips.

          NOTTINGHAM
They could at least use decent wine.

INT. JOHN'S CASTLE HALL - DAY

John swallows wine. Cogsworth tries to refill the empty glass. John jerks it away, gaping at Nottingham.

          JOHN
All of it?

Cogsworth dances around John. He misses the glass and dribbles on the floor. Nottingham shuffles his feet and MUMBLES.

          JOHN
What?

          NOTTINGHAM
They left the vegetables.

          JOHN
They took silver? Steel? Meat?

Nottingham nods. Cogsworth gets a glurg into John's glass.

>   NOTTINGHAM
> We've got a lot of squash.

John blinks, then tosses off the last of his wine—except the glass is full. Wine splashes in his face.

>   JOHN
> Cogsworth!

Cogsworth grabs the glass and pats him with a cloth. John rips it away and rubs his face.

>   JOHN
>   (to Nottingham)
> Longchamp will nail your jewels to the wall.

Nottingham studies the ceiling.

>   NOTTINGHAM
> He told me to leave the Church alone.

John's eyes narrow.

>   NOTTINGHAM
> I didn't mention you.

John takes a breath and lets it out slowly.

>   JOHN
> I owe you for that. But someday those hypocrites will have to be taken on.

Nottingham shrugs.

NOTTINGHAM
Render unto—

JOHN
Don't give me salad. They're undercutting honest merchants.

Nottingham looks back at the ceiling.

Cogsworth tries to give John another glass of wine. John throws the cloth at him and heads outside. Nottingham takes the glass.

EXT. JOHN'S CASTLE YARD

Nottingham follows John out. A SNEERING PRISONER stands on a scaffold beyond them, next to a noose. The Executioner stumbles about, arms waving, peering uncertainly.

JOHN
Longchamp has reports on Robin. He must be stopped.

Nottingham looks uncertain which one he means.

JOHN
For a thief, Robin is rather colorful.

Nottingham sips. The Executioner happens on the rope. He smiles in delight and wanders on, waving his free hand.

JOHN
They say he's a splendid bowman.

Nottingham spews wine all over. Cogsworth dashes outside and grabs his glass.

JOHN
Quite vain about it, too. And a master of disguise.

The Executioner tries vainly to put the noose over a post in the corner of the scaffold.

NOTTINGHAM
M'lord. He's the worst shot since the invention of the bow.

JOHN
So I thought perhaps a contest. Longchamp agreed.

John smiles into the distance. Nottingham sputters. The Prisoner grabs the rope from the Executioner and tosses it over his own head. The Executioner stumbles toward him.

NOTTINGHAM
He'll never come. He's—

JOHN
We'll have it here.

EXECUTIONER
Wait I—

Nottingham gapes. The Prisoner sneers at the Executioner and flips the lever. He crashes to the ground below.

EXECUTIONER
—haven't tied it.

The Prisoner sits up groggily. The Executioner blunders through the trap door and lands on the Prisoner's head.

> JOHN
> One month.

Nottingham bows marginally and stumbles toward his horse. The Executioner stands. An ASSISTANT checks the Prisoner.

> ASSISTANT
> Dead. Broken neck.

> EXECUTIONER
> Oh, my. Oh, dear. That's terrible.

> JOHN
> Spread the word.

The Assistant consoles the Executioner. Nottingham mounts and rides off, shaking his head.

EXT. FOREST CAMP - DAY

Tuck shakes his head while munching a huge sandwich. Robin practices bow. Marian walks by and slaps the sandwich out of Tuck's hands.

> MARIAN
> It's the twelfth century. Sandwiches!

Tuck watches ants descend on his lunch.

> TUCK
> Almost the thirteenth.

An arrow THWACKS into the bull's-eye.

> ROBIN
>
> Yes!

Marian and Tuck swivel toward the target. John Little GRUNTS.

> JOHN LITTLE
>
> A million monkeys in a million years.

> ROBIN
>
> You wait. I'll be ready.

He swaggers to the target and collects a half dozen arrows; the rest are in the outer rings, except for one in the target's leg.

> TUCK
>
> Lad's got dedication.

> MARIAN
>
> Lad's got no coordination. But he sang like a bird, till Mother cured him of it.

Tuck looks at her.

> MARIAN
>
> 'Tweren't manly enough.

She whips up her crossbow and nails a bull's-eye right over Robin's shoulder. He jumps back and glares at her.

> MARIAN
>
> It's not a contest. It's a trap, you dough-brain.

                    ROBIN
Frog farts. You'd see conspiracy in the College of
Cardinals.

                    MARIAN
Exactly.

Tuck nods sadly.

EXT. OUTSIDE JOHN'S CASTLE - DAY

Pavilions color the landscape. Huge CROWDS
chatter and laugh, milling from FOOD VENDORS
to JUGGLERS to ACROBATS.

MEN and WOMEN practice bow at a score of
targets. LADS snatch arrows from the targets and
race them back to the shooters.

One BOY darts in front of a target. Fourteen arrows
sprout from his body. Two other BOYS pick up his
body and toss him on a PILE of other arrow-studded
bodies.

Longchamp clucks his tongue and turns to King
Richard.

                    LONGCHAMP
Enough boys?

Richard nods.

                    RICHARD
Survival of the fit. Good to help Mother Nature
when we can.

Longchamp nods and turns back to watch the practice. Count John looks sick. He starts to leave.

> RICHARD
> Splendid idea, brother. I love a good contest.

John cancels his departure.

> JOHN
> Nice of you to visit. We don't see much of you in England.

Richard CHUCKLES.

> RICHARD
> Ah, England. Land of revenue and cannon fodder. How could I ever retake France without the English?

> JOHN
> Cannons haven't been invented yet.

> LONGCHAMP
> Church has many canons.

Richard and Longchamp laugh. John grins weakly and leaves.

EXT. TARGET RANGE

A FAT MAN fires his bow; the arrow THUDS into the target. A SKINNY MAN fires; his arrow hits closer.

Marian wears a fake mustache and hides her hair under a cap. Robin sports a false gray beard, at odds with his hair color.

MARIAN
They're looking for you. Don't win.

ROBIN
Ah, Marian. Don't worry.

He saunters toward the firing line. Marian looks around, then slips over to the bushes beside the range.

Near Marian, six-year-old LISA struggles to draw a longbow, holding it sideways. Marian looks around, then dashes out and shows the girl to angle the shot at forty-five degrees. Lisa fires, the arrow wobbles up, and . . . bull's-eye.

John smiles at the shot, then frowns as Marian sneaks back toward the bushes. He looks around, and heads toward Nottingham.

Robin studies his target and draws. His bow shudders, then steadies. He takes a deep breath. A MOSQUITO bites his hand. He twitches as he fires.

ROBIN
Ow.

The Fat Man watches.

FAT MAN
Rotate your elbow.

The arrow hits near center. Robin searches his hand.

The CROWD mills around as disgruntled CONTESTANTS duck under the RED TAPE around the shooting area. Nottingham goes from one loser to another and stares into each face.

Longchamp stops him.

> LONGCHAMP
> What doing? Winners—

> NOTTINGHAM
> Robin couldn't win a bath if he fell in the English Channel.

Longchamp glowers. Nottingham keeps searching.

EXT. TARGET RANGE - LATER

The Fat Man fires, hitting near center.

Marian sees Nottingham checking losers.

The Skinny Man fires, doing poorly. He SWEARS.

Marian pushes into the Crowd, fighting to get near Robin.

Nottingham and Marian see each other. Nottingham frowns, then his eyes go wide. Marian ducks and pushes away. Nottingham struggles through the Crowd after her.

A PIGEON flies over the target area.

Lisa fires her wobbly shot. The arrow just misses the Pigeon. It SQUAWKS and drops some poop.

Robin fires. He grimaces.

The pigeon poop hits Robin's arrow; it shudders, alters direction, and THUDS into the bull's-eye. Robin gapes.

Nottingham paces on the edge of the Crowd, looking around. Marian is nowhere in sight. He looks back at the castle.

The Pigeon lands on a castle tower and SQUAWKS.

EXT. TARGET RANGE - LATER

Cogsworth walks onto the field.

> COGSWORTH
> The finalists are Lisa of Knight's Bridge and Loxley of Bagel.

The Crowd cheers.

> COGSWORTH
> And now to the wall, for the final shoot-off.

The Crowd keeps cheering. Robin and Lisa are swept toward the castle.

EXT. JOHN'S CASTLE YARD

The Crowd boils through the gate into the open yard. Marian breaks away, races up stone stairs, and hides behind some water barrels.

EXT. CASTLE FRONT WALL

John leads Richard, Longchamp, Robin, Lisa, Cogsworth, and a few GUARDS with a target, up stone steps to the top of the front wall.

John, Richard, and Longchamp step aside as the target is set up. They lean on water barrels near where Marian hides.

> RICHARD
> Robin Hood wins, right?

> JOHN
> Well . . .

> LONGCHAMP
> Exactly.

Richard looks at Robin and Lisa.

> RICHARD
> Why don't you just arrest him now?

John looks thoughtful.

> LONGCHAMP
> Which? Master of disguise.

Richard and John give him a funny look. Richard shrugs.

> RICHARD
> So shoot 'em both.

John looks horrified. He looks away, then blinks and smiles, gesturing at the Crowd.

> LONGCHAMP
> Exelle—

> JOHN
> And disappoint your people?

Longchamp looks irate. Richard nods.

                RICHARD
Good thinking.

Johns smiles. Longchamp scowls.

                LONGCHAMP
Whichever. Won't get away.

Richard chuckles. He and Longchamp move off. John follows.

Marian dashes the other way, past an absent-minded GUARD, and onto the side wall.

She pulls a piece of wood from one leg of her pants, and a thin bar of metal from the other, held in a curve with a steel wire. She snaps them together crossways.

EXT. JOHN'S CASTLE YARD

Nottingham looks up at the front wall. The target is ready. He shakes his head and wanders among the Crowd, peering at faces.

EXT. CASTLE FRONT WALL

Cogsworth flips a COIN. At the height of its arc, Nottingham's Raven snatches it.

                COGSWORTH
Hey!

EXT. TOP OF TOWER

The Raven lands on the tower at the end of the wall, beside the Pigeon. The Pigeon SQUAWKS and side-steps. The Raven sets down the coin.

>RAVEN
>Po bird. Not po.

The Raven looks at the coin.

>RAVEN
>Tails.

EXT. CASTLE FRONT WALL

John signals Cogsworth to get on with it.

>COGSWORTH
>Tails. Mr. of-Bagel, you shoot first.

Robin shakes as he looks from John to Richard.

EXT. CASTLE SIDE WALL

Marian snaps a stock onto her growing crossbow.

EXT. CASTLE FRONT WALL

Robin takes a deep breath.

>LISA
>Don't be nervous. The trophy's only silver.

He smiles weakly at the girl. He starts to draw.

> LISA
And rotate your elbow.

He twists his bow arm and looks back at her. She smiles like an angel. He lets out a breath, and suddenly grins.

> ROBIN
Thanks, kid.

He looks back at the target, holds his breath, and gets suddenly still. He fires.

Bull's-eye. A hair above dead center.

Robin slowly lowers his bow arm, staring in shock. Richard leans near Longchamp.

> RICHARD
Now?

Longchamp shakes his head. Cogsworth gestures Lisa forward.

EXT. CASTLE SIDE WALL

Marian slaps a metal bolt into the firing groove of her crossbow. She raises it and aims at Lisa.

EXT. TOP OF TOWER

The Raven hops toward the Pigeon.

> RAVEN
Pretty bird?

The Pigeon SQUAWKS and takes off, dropping more poop.

            RAVEN
    Stinky bird.

EXT. CASTLE FRONT WALL

Cogsworth dodges the pigeon poop. Lisa half-draws her horizontal bow, angles her aim upwards, and fires.

EXT. CASTLE SIDE WALL

Marian tracks the wobbly arrow's glacial path. The Pigeon SQUAWKS and snatches the arrow with its claws. Marian sits up.

            MARIAN
    Sot.

EXT. JOHN'S CASTLE YARD

Nottingham looks up at the sound and sees Marian.

EXT. CASTLE SIDE WALL

Marian fires. The wire rips off her mustache. The bolt streaks away.

It glances off the Pigeon's head, stunning it.

The Pigeon falls toward the target, clutching Lisa's arrow.

EXT. JOHN'S CASTLE YARD

Nottingham races toward Marian's side wall.

EXT. CASTLE FRONT WALL

Lisa's arrow, Pigeon in tow, slices through Robin's arrow and punctures the target dead center. The Pigeon dangles below, claws still tight on the shaft.

      COGSWORTH
The winner.

He points to Lisa. She gapes at the Pigeon, about to cry. Longchamp points at her as well.

      LONGCHAMP
Robin Hood. Arrest.

The Guards shove Robin out of the way and dash toward Lisa. She stares at all the Guards. The Pigeon drops.

      LISA
I didn't mean to kill it.

Robin backs away. The Guards grab Lisa.

The Pigeon staggers to its feet, one wing to its head, and weaves away.

EXT. JOHN'S CASTLE YARD

Nottingham dashes up the stone stairs.

      NOTTINGHAM
Marian. You're under arrest.

EXT. CASTLE SIDE WALL

Marian jerks her crossbow at Nottingham, then hesitates and looks toward Robin.

> MARIAN
> Robin. Jump.

Nottingham smashes into Marian. Her crossbow goes flying.

EXT. CASTLE FRONT WALL

Robin looks toward Marian for a microsecond.

> ROBIN
> Okay.

He turns and dives over the outside wall.

John looks from Marian to Robin, then runs to the edge and looks over. The Guards rush to the edge, holding Lisa in the air. Richard glares at Longchamp.

EXT. OUTSIDE CASTLE

Robin lands in a wagon full of fresh cess-pit dredgings. He clambers out and jumps on a horse Tuck holds for him.

> ROBIN
> You came, my belov—

> TUCK
> Shut up.

John shakes a fist.

JOHN
Robin Hood.

The Crowd boils from the castle, blocking the Guards from leaving.

TUCK
You stink.

ROBIN
I should have won.

He and Tuck ride off. The Crowd CHEERS.

SKINNY MAN
Told you he'd come.

FAT MAN
I knew he'd win.

The Guards push vainly at the back of the Crowd.

EXT. CASTLE SIDE WALL

Nottingham and Marian wrestle, slowing with exhaustion. A BEARDED GUARD and GAUNT GUARD run up. They hover on the edge of the fight. The Bearded Guard picks up Marian's crossbow.

NOTTINGHAM
Give up.

MARIAN
You couldn't beat an egg.

She kicks. He grabs her foot and tosses her back. He dives toward her. She leaps up and flings him into some barrels.

The Bearded Guard knocks her on the back of the head with her crossbow. She collapses, out cold.

Nottingham jumps up. He picks up the Bearded Guard and throws him over the wall, then kneels and checks Marian.

The Gaunt Guard runs to the wall and looks down.

> GAUNT GUARD
> Eeooo.

Nottingham wraps a cloth around Marian's head, looking worried.

> NOTTINGHAM
> Get the leech.

He caresses her ear.

INT. JOHN'S CASTLE HALL - DAY

Richard stalks toward the outside door. Longchamp races behind, taking notes on a scroll. John slowly follows.

> LONGCHAMP
> Ten thousand pikes, a dozen bandages . . .

Richard yanks open the door and pauses, looking back at John.

RICHARD
I can't believe you let Robin Hood get away.

LONGCHAMP
(muttering)
Treason. Foul plotting. Underhanded—

RICHARD
Shut up, Longchamp.

JOHN
We have his sister. We'll find him.

Richard blinks.

RICHARD
Marian? Incest, too?

He looks at Longchamp, who shrugs and writes notes.

JOHN
No. That's a vile—

RICHARD
Never mind. Just get me those Irish troops.

Richard crooks a finger at Longchamp, and the two of them march out, slamming the door. John stares at the door.

JOHN
Robin supports this guy. The church supports this guy. All England loves this guy.

He shakes his head.

JOHN
If they like him, they'd bloody worship me.

He shrugs and turns away.

JOHN
Well, not the church. Not the peasants. Maybe not the nobles.

He pauses, one hand on the door to his study.

JOHN
Other than that, I'd be real popular.

He opens the door.

INT. DUNGEON - LATER

A SOLDIER opens a cell door. Hinges SQUEAL. Cogsworth enters the cell, carrying a tray with a loaf of bread and carafe of water.

INT. CELL

Marian sits on a cot, one wrist chained to the wall, one ankle chained to the floor, and a bandage around her head. A torch casts flickering shadows.

MARIAN
Another interrogator? How many you got?

Cogsworth waves at the Soldier, who locks the door. STEPS recede. Cogsworth sets the tray beside Marian.

COGSWORTH
I see you broke Nottingham's nose.

She grabs the bread and tears off a hunk.

>   MARIAN
>   No file?

Cogsworth sighs.

>   COGSWORTH
>   He needs you, Marian.

>   MARIAN
>   I wouldn't help that satanic killer if he burned me
>   alive.

She pauses, bread halfway to her mouth.

>   MARIAN
>   He can't do that, can he?

Cogsworth shakes his head.

>   COGSWORTH
>   He can only hang you.

>   MARIAN
>   Thank God.

She stuffs the bread in her mouth.

>   COGSWORTH
>   He . . . Nottingham didn't use sorcery.

Marian stops chewing and narrows her eyes.
Cogsworth shuffles back a step.

>   COGSWORTH
>   He didn't even hang that girl.

Marian spits out the bread.

> MARIAN
> Who bribed you?

> COGSWORTH
> Only you!

He looks around, fidgeting, then back at Marian.

> COGSWORTH
> Nottingham's guards? John's, really.

She nods. Cogsworth flips open his notebook.

> COGSWORTH
> I overheard Sergeant Porkers.

INT. JOHN'S CASTLE - DAY - FLASHBACK

Porkers salutes Count John in the cavernous hall. Cogsworth cleans tapestries on the wall behind them.

> PORKERS
> Correct sir. We put the girl's clothes on the body. He sent her to Ireland.

John laughs, to Porkers's relief.

> JOHN
> How soggy. He'd never make a leader.

Porkers looks down and scuffs a toe. John studies him.

> JOHN
> Or he'd make a really good one.

Porkers gives him a searching look.

INT. CELL - RETURN

Cogsworth shuts the notebook and huddles nervously. Marian gapes. Suddenly she laughs and throws a piece of bread at him.

> MARIAN
> That idiot. Now the church hates him worse'n they hate John.

Cogsworth relaxes and smiles slightly.

> MARIAN
> All right. Tell him I'll talk to him.

Cogsworth smiles openly.

> MARIAN
> But I won't help him find Robin. He won't get out of hanging *me*.

Cogsworth's smile evaporates.

> COGSWORTH
> Ah. Well, that shoots the other plan.

He stuffs away the notebook and starts to leave.

> MARIAN
> What other plan?

He hesitates, then BANGS on the door.

> COGSWORTH
> No, no. You've made up your mind.

The door CREAKS open. Marian rattles her shackles.

> MARIAN
> What other plan, you horse apple?

He pauses at the door, then shakes his head.

> COGSWORTH
> You'd just get mad.

The door MOANS shut.

> MARIAN
> Come back here, you Tory!

The key CLICKS in the lock.

INT. DUNGEON - DAY

Nottingham drums his fingers on a table at the end of a hall, a thick bandage on his nose. An AGED JAILER drags Marian to a chair and chains her ankle and wrist to it.

> AGED JAILER
> If that's all, m'lord?

> NOTTINGHAM
> Yes, catch up with John. Tell him "good hunting."

The Aged Jailer hands Nottingham a key and withdraws. Nottingham pockets the key and watches Marian. She stares back. He draws a breath.

> NOTTINGHAM
> You know you're in deep kimchee.

>   MARIAN
> Tough. You can't burn me.

>   NOTTINGHAM
> Tell me where —-

>   MARIAN
> Can't boil me in oil.

He looks sick.

>   NOTTINGHAM
> —where Robin—

>   MARIAN
> Or put me on the rack. Or rip off my fingernails.

He slaps his hand on the table, swallowing hard.

>   NOTTINGHAM
> I can bloody well—

>   MARIAN
> Can't draw and quarter me, either.

Nottingham covers his ears.

>   MARIAN
> Or dice me into hors d'oeuvres and deliver me
> with dry wine.

He leaps up and backs away.

>   NOTTINGHAM
> Stop.

MARIAN
All you can do is dangle me on the end of a rope.

She puts her free hand on her throat and makes CHOKING NOISES. Nottingham races up a circular stairwell, hands over his ears.

NOTTINGHAM
Shut up. Shut up. Shut up.

Marian looks thoughtful at the sound of CRASHING STONES. She snags a nail off the floor and fiddles with her handcuff.

Nottingham comes back down the steps, brushing off stone dust. Marian hides the nail. He pauses when he sees her, but she doesn't say anything. He resumes his seat.

NOTTINGHAM
I need some suggestions.

She raises an eyebrow.

MARIAN
Why'd you capture me?

NOTTINGHAM
Why'd you let Robin compete?

MARIAN
Why'd you hold the contest?

NOTTINGHAM
Why'd you turn into a thief?

                    MARIAN
Why did you?

Nottingham sputters.

                    NOTTINGHAM
I'm a—

                    MARIAN
Tax collector.

He works his mouth a few times, then looks away.

                    NOTTINGHAM
I had reasons.

Marian slips the nail back into the keyhole on her handcuff.

                    MARIAN
I heard about your redhead.

Nottingham gets up and paces.

                    NOTTINGHAM
Look, examples have to be made.

He pulls off his nose bandage and scoops a spider off the wall.

                    NOTTINGHAM
I have a job to do.

Marian's handcuff snaps open with a soft CLICK. She leans down and works on her ankle.

                    NOTTINGHAM
If you're not ruthless, people rebel. Then more of
them die.

He releases the spider at a barred window.

                    MARIAN
Really?

                    NOTTINGHAM
That's what Richard—

His Raven lands on the window ledge and eats the
spider. Nottingham slams his fist and turns back.
Marian sits up quickly.

                    NOTTINGHAM
Yes. Really.

                    MARIAN
And you're ruthless?

                    NOTTINGHAM
Yes.

He leans over her.

                    NOTTINGHAM
Now tell me where—

                    MARIAN
Ireland, wasn't it?

Nottingham blinks.

                    MARIAN
Your redhead.

Nottingham's face goes slack. He falls into his chair.

> NOTTINGHAM
> Who told you?

They stare at each other a moment.

> NOTTINGHAM
> I'm a failure.

Nottingham puts his head down. Marian studies him.

> NOTTINGHAM
> I can't stop taxes. I can't help anyone.

She frowns.

> NOTTINGHAM
> I sold the manor, and all the animals I could pass off as pets. Paid tax for a hundred families so I wouldn't have to kick anyone out.

Her eyes go wide. She slowly nods once.

> NOTTINGHAM
> If I sell any more, they'll be slaughtered for food.

Marian rises and walks around the table.

> NOTTINGHAM
> I kept hoping it would get better. That someday . . . . But it never will. Not while Richard's around.

She massages his shoulders.

NOTTINGHAM
And then you called off our wedding.

He suddenly sits up.

NOTTINGHAM
Wait a minute. I never proposed.

MARIAN
I did.

He looks confused.

MARIAN
We were nine.

He slumps, smiling faintly.

NOTTINGHAM
You damn near broke my arm.

MARIAN
But you agreed.

NOTTINGHAM
A promise under duress—

MARIAN
It's still the twelfth century. Your word is your honor.

He chuckles. Then his eyes widen and he spins, grabbing her arms, looking from her to the chair.

She pulls him to his feet and wraps her arms around him.

> MARIAN
> You have trapped me.

He frowns.

> MARIAN
> Made me your prisoner.

> NOTTINGHAM
> I'm not really into bondage.

She clutches his jaw. His mouth goes fishy.

> MARIAN
> Now kill me.

She kisses him violently. After a moment, she breaks and stares him in the eye.

> MARIAN
> Take me, or hang me. I don't care. But don't you dare let me go.

One of her hands drops. He goes up on tiptoe, gasping. He gets a gleam in his eye, then bends and kisses her back. They sink to the floor.

INT. DUNGEON - LATER

Torchlight flickers. A mound of straw shudders and a leg sticks out. An arm follows. Nottingham and Marian sit up.

> NOTTINGHAM
> I'm going to have lice in all the wrong places.

She throws a handful of straw at him.

MARIAN
So put some in the "right" places.

He rolls away and stands, straightening his clothes.

NOTTINGHAM
I've got a plan. You got me thinking.

MARIAN
So nice to be of service.

She snatches loose clothing and enters an open cell.

NOTTINGHAM
Seriously. See, I don't need to catch Robin. You're doing my job for me.

She sticks her head out of the cell.

NOTTINGHAM
Not my job. My real job, the one I'd like to be doing.

She blinks and disappears.

MARIAN (O.S.)
Crystalline, as always.

NOTTINGHAM
You're taking money that would be taxes, right?

MARIAN (O.S.)
Sometimes.

NOTTINGHAM
Yeah. Then what do you do?

Marian comes out, dressed.

> MARIAN
> Give it—

> NOTTINGHAM
> —to the taxed. Then I take it.

> MARIAN
> And I take it.

> NOTTINGHAM
> And you give it back. Full circle.

She grins.

> NOTTINGHAM
> Count John would love it, if I dared tell him.

Marian steps to her chair and flicks her handcuff.

> MARIAN
> What about this?

Nottingham shrugs.

> NOTTINGHAM
> You get rescued. Who's your spy? Cogsworth?

Marian gapes.

> NOTTINGHAM
> I'm not completely stupid.

She snorts and takes a torch off the wall. She paces.

MARIAN
But we can't communicate if he's compromised.

NOTTINGHAM
True. He could let me know where you were, so I search other places.

Marian wanders behind him.

MARIAN
Exactly. So I should break out by myself.

Nottingham pauses, staring in the distance. A dim THUD comes from the stairs above.

NOTTINGHAM
But how . . . ?

Marian bashes him over the head with the torch. He collapses, out cold. She throws the torch aside, kneels, and bats out a tiny flame in his hair. She caresses an ear.

MARIAN
Now we're even, lover.

John Little clatters down the spiral stairs, sword in one hand, large stone in the other.

JOHN LITTLE
Someone's got a violent version of a twelve-step program.

He catches sight of Marian.

JOHN LITTLE
Hey. Get back in your cell.

Marian looks up at him. He reaches bottom.

              JOHN LITTLE
          We're busting you out.

              MARIAN
          Sorry. Already out.

He tosses the stone aside and takes a step toward
Nottingham.

              JOHN LITTLE
          He need finishing?

              MARIAN
          No! I mean, leave him.

John Little raises an eyebrow, but follows her to the
spiral stairs. Robin's head appears above.

              ROBIN
          Hurry, you two.

Marian pauses and looks at John Little.

              MARIAN
          I'm impressed.

              JOHN LITTLE
          Tuck brought him.

              MARIAN
          Ah.

They scurry up the stairs.

INT. DUNGEON - LATER

Longchamp stands beside an open cell door in John's dungeon. He glares from cell to John to Nottingham to cell, then whaps Nottingham's head bandage.

EXT. WOODS - DAY

Marian and Robin's Band stops a lone COURIER in the colorful autumn woods. They take his pouch.

EXT. WOODS - DAY

WINTER: Nottingham and his twenty Guards wait in ambush along a snowy trail. No one comes. Porkers idly flips a coin.

EXT. WOODS - DAY

Deep green coats the trees of summer. Marian and company stop a carriage with three NOBLE LADIES. The ladies try to vamp Tuck, till Robin puts an arm around him. Tuck shoves off the arm.

INT. JOHN'S CASTLE HALL - DAY

Longchamp rants at Count John, waving a sheaf of papers and pointing at Nottingham, standing to the side. John spreads his hands, palms up.

EXT. WOODS - DAY

Cogsworth leads Nottingham from his Guards. Curly-Hair sneers. Cogsworth and Nottingham go through brilliant fall woods to a quiet pond, where Marian awaits.

Nottingham approaches tentatively, rubbing the back of his head. Marian jumps him, tickling and laughing.

INT. STUDY - DAY

Longchamp enters a room where Curly-Hair waits. Curly-Hair turns from the snow-lined window. Longchamp tosses him a small pouch. Curly-Hair JINGLES it and SNICKERS. Longchamp unrolls a map on a large table.

EXT. FOREST - DAY

Early spring flowers bloom. Nottingham waits beside a river. Marian approaches. Nottingham rises and gives her a present. She opens it and lifts out a silk dress. She raises an eyebrow, then smiles.

EXT. FOREST - LATER

Marian poses in her silk dress beside the river. Nottingham shudders, then tears off his sword belt and attacks. He swings her through the air; she laughs.

He sets her down. They kiss.

Longchamp and two score KNIGHTS burst from the trees.

> LONGCHAMP
> Treason. Yes!

The Knights race around Nottingham and Marian. He twists toward his sword, then stops. It's too far away.

Longchamp motions the Knights to close in. Nottingham shoves Marian down, grabs her ankles, and whirls her around. The Knights skitter back, gaping as her dress flies up.

NOTTINGHAM
You'll never take her alive.

MARIAN
What? Put me DOWWWWwwwwwwwwwwwwwn—

He tosses her over the Knights. She SPLASHES into the river and is swept away downstream. The Knights grab Nottingham.

MARIAN
(spluttering)
You'll . . . pay for . . . that.

Marian disappears around a bend. Longchamp glares.

LONGCHAMP
Couldn't agree more.

He slugs Nottingham in the belly, then winces, clutching his hand. Nottingham hardly budges. The Knights drag him away.

INT. JOHN'S CASTLE STUDY - DAY

John finishes a sit-up. He rises and pounds a fist on his belly.

JOHN
Nothing like keeping fit, what?

Longchamp rubs the splint on his hand. John sits down at his desk.

>   LONGCHAMP
> Nottingham's sentence—

>   JOHN
>   No.

John dips a pen and starts writing.

>   LONGCHAMP
> Delay not right.

>   JOHN
> Tough crusaders.

Longchamp slams his splint on John's desk.

>   LONGCHAMP
> Death warrant signed.

Longchamp winces, shaking his hand. John looks down at the squiggle in the letter he was writing. His eyes narrow.

>   LONGCHAMP
> I mean . . . have authority . . . .

John studies him, then sets down his pen.

>   JOHN
> Executions of nobles must be confirmed by the king.

LONGCHAMP
Unless not reached in thirty days. Then mine. No way get word from France—

John stands; his chair falls. Longchamp licks his lips.

JOHN
One more time. Slowly. Thirty days. Or it's murder.

Longchamp swallows, then nods.

LONGCHAMP
Fine. Let stew. I wait.

He sweeps out the door. John watches it slam and chews his lip. A KNOCK comes behind him. He spins. A hidden door in his bookcase swings open. Marian steps through.

MARIAN
Alone now?

JOHN
How did you . . . ?

Cogsworth follows her in.

COGSWORTH
Sorry, sire. The front door seemed a bit presumptuous.

John looks from one to the other.

COGSWORTH
You did say you'd finally consider plotting.

John hesitates a moment longer, then bolts for the main door Longchamp went through.

Marian looks at Cogsworth. She dives for the hidden door. Cogsworth grabs her arm.

> COGSWORTH
> Too late. He knows where it lets out.

She glares at him, then pulls a knife and crouches beside the main door, peeking around the edge. A candle sputters.

INT. JOHN'S CASTLE STUDY - LATER

A shorter candle sputters. John pops through the hidden door and shuts the bookcase.

> JOHN
> He's gone. You weren't followed.

He sees Marian and raises an eyebrow. She stands, stares at him a moment, then fumbles the knife back into its sheath.

> MARIAN
> I . . . uh . . . sorry.

> COGSWORTH
> Good choice of entrance, sire.

> JOHN
> Don't call me that.

He looks from Cogsworth to Marian.

JOHN
You have a plan?

Marian looks at Cogsworth. He nods. She takes a
breath.

MARIAN
Nottingham said it. Things will never get better as
long as Richard is king.

JOHN
Not to mention your lover getting the worse for
wear.

She blushes.

COGSWORTH
It's tight, but there's a chance. Richard is laying
siege to Chalus-Chabrol.

He pulls out two scrolls and lays them down one at a
time.

COGSWORTH
This one gets her through the English lines. And
this one she uses first, to see Philip.

John looks at him a moment, then picks up the
second scroll.

JOHN
It says he gets to keep all the French land he
currently holds.

Cogsworth nods.

INT. FRENCH CASTLE HALL - DAY

Marian, dressed as a soldier, is surrounded by French PIKEMEN. One holds her crossbow. Philip sits behind an ornate desk and reads a scroll.

>   PHILIP
> Even the former Plantagenet conquests. Once John is king.

He squints at Marian.

>   PHILIP
> Just for giving you a free hand? Even if you fail?

>   MARIAN
> John is an Englishman, your majesty. Unlike his father or Richard, he has no interest in depleting the treasury claiming France.

Philip stares at her, then goes back to studying the scroll.

>   PHILIP
> And what's with the deadline? Why do I have to decide so fast?

>   MARIAN
> It's . . . personal, m'lord.

Philip frowns. His AIDE frowns more harshly, and signals the pikemen. Marian lets them drag her to the door.

>   PHILIP
> Wait.

He looks from the scroll to Marian, then grabs a pen and signs it. He thrusts it at his Aide.

PHILIP
Too good to pass up. Get this to Rome.

He stands and walks up to Marian. The pikemen move aside. He grabs her crossbow from one and hands it to her.

PHILIP
I have no idea what you are planning, young lady. But you'd better not miss.

She hesitates, smiles, and fakes a curtsy in her trousers.

INT. DUNGEON CELL - DAY

Nottingham sits on the stone floor, chained to the wall, his bruised body barely covered by filthy rags. Longchamp brandishes a torch in his face. Nottingham squints.

LONGCHAMP
Fourteen days gone. Eighteen left.

NOTTINGHAM
You're grasp of mathematics is exemplary.

Longchamp leans forward and grabs Nottingham by his rags.

LONGCHAMP
Exemp . . . ?

> NOTTINGHAM
> Aren't you afraid I might have a knife?

Longchamp leaps back. Nottingham laughs. Longchamp glares.

> LONGCHAMP
> Guard.

A GUARD enters. Longchamp points at Nottingham.

> LONGCHAMP
> Remove clothes. Concealing something.

The Guard looks at him askance.

EXT. OUTSIDE FRENCH CASTLE - NIGHT

Hundreds of campfires surround the castle of Chalus-Chabrol on a moonlit night. Marian huddles behind a bush, watching the castle beyond the nearby ENGLISH TROOPS.

She takes a breath, jams her hair under a helmet, and pulls a scroll from her belt pouch. She starts to stand, then huddles down and holds the scroll up to the moonlight.

> MARIAN
> Sot.

She stuffs the scroll back in her pouch, pulls out another, and checks it. She stands, brushes off a leaf, and walks forward.

A SENTRY sees her and rushes over, brandishing a spear.

SENTRY
Halt. Goes who there?

MARIAN
"Who goes there."

An OFFICER walks toward them.

SENTRY
What? I asked first.

MARIAN
You got it wrong. It's supposed to be—

The Officer grabs the Sentry's spear and levels it at Marian.

OFFICER
I had a grammar teacher once. Just once.

Marian freezes, then holds out the scroll. The Officer hands the spear to the Sentry and grabs the scroll.

OFFICER
To whom it may concern . . . bearer . . .

After a moment he snorts and jabs it back at Marian.

OFFICER
You tell Richard our morale is fine, but it won't be if he sends spies checking on us.

Marian nods quickly, hiding a swallow. She clutches the scroll and heads into the midst of the English Troops.

EXT. BASE OF CASTLE WALL - LATER

Marian looks over her shoulder at the last of the English troops, and darts amongst boulders at the base of the castle wall. She stuffs the scroll in her belt pouch and pulls out the other one.

She clambers over rocks, looking up at the castle now and then. She frowns, studies the wall, and keeps moving.

She sees a white stone in the wall, reflecting moonlight. She glances over her shoulder again, then heads toward the wall. She feels around and finds a button. She pushes it.

A doorbell CHIMES. Marian flinches and looks back toward the English lines. A couple of voices YELL incoherently, and three shapes race by, outlined by campfires.

A line of light outlines a door opening behind Marian. A HAND reaches out, grabs her by the scruff of the neck, and hauls her inside. The door THUDS shut.

INT. STONE HALL

Marian lays on the floor, pinned by a dozen swords and spears, helmet beside her. French SOLDIERS point at her hair.

A French MAJOR reads her scroll. He BARKS a command and the soldiers stand aside. One helps Marian up. The Major glances from the note to her. He eyes her up and down.

MAJOR
What did you do for Philip to get a note like this?

Marian slugs him in the gut. Two soldiers grab her. The Major waves them away. He looks at Marian.

MAJOR
That is an answer I can trust.

Marian glares at him a moment, then nods.

MARIAN
I don't have much time.

MAJOR
March twenty-sixth, come the dawn. But the rains are over for now.

Marian's mouth tightens.

INT. DUNGEON CELL - DAY

Nottingham slumps nude in his chains. Longchamp stalks in with a torch.

LONGCHAMP
Eighteen down, nine more. Not matter if answer. Richard never spare you.

Nottingham barely lifts his head. His speech blurs.

NOTTINGHAM
Wha . . . djou say . . . ?

Longchamp growls and steps closer.

                    LONGCHAMP
        You not cheat death, stinking—

Nottingham's bleary face gets cross-eyed.

                    NOTTINGHAM
        What? Whatjou say?

Longchamp leans down and grabs his hair, twisting
his head up to stare him in the face.

                    LONGCHAMP
        Said—

A slender stream of WATER shoots up and splashes
Longchamp in the nose. He lets go and leaps back
with a SHOUT. Nottingham looks fully alert.

                    NOTTINGHAM
        Oh, my. I'm terribly sorry.

Longchamp spits and backs further.

                    LONGCHAMP
        Guard. Clothes. Conceal.

EXT. OUTSIDE FRENCH CASTLE - DAY

Thousands of English TROOPS encircle Chalus-
Chabrol. Large tents surround a giant banner of a lion
rampant. Nearby Troops cook, polish leather, carry
buckets, and don armor.

High on the castle wall, centered above the main gate,
a single French crossbow ARCHER appears.

The bustle in the English camp continues. After a moment, a LIEUTENANT notices the French Archer. The Lieutenant grabs the Sentry and points at the Archer.

> LIEUTENANT
> Wake up. Keep their heads down.

The Sentry drops his pike and grabs a longbow. He draws and fires. The French Archer ignores the shaft.

> LIEUTENANT
> Again.

The Sentry fires. Several more arrows arc toward the Archer from around the English camp. All miss, though one nearly grazes the Archer's helmet. The Archer ignores them all.

Several troops gather around the Sentry, looking up. A CAPTAIN stomps up in a fancy uniform and barks at them.

> CAPTAIN
> What's going on?

The Lieutenant points at the Archer, looking exasperated, and walks away. The Captain looks up.

On the wall, the French Archer watches back. Occasional arrows smash into the battlements or sail high. French CHEERING begins.

> CAPTAIN
> Bloody hell. Lieuten— Where'd he go?

He looks around. Several OFFICERS join the throng watching the lone French Archer. The Captain shoves them aside and stomps toward the largest tent, MUTTERING, face livid. He shoves open the flap and bellows.

> CAPTAIN
> Richard. Your Majesty. We've got a problem.

He looks back. Few arrows fly. The French Archer mounts the battlements, in full view from helmet to boots. A crossbow dangles from one hand. A few English laugh, and some cheer.

Richard comes out of his tent wearing a coarse undershirt, leg armor, and a scowl.

> RICHARD
> What is it?

He throws a towel back toward his tent and follows the Captain's finger to the castle wall. He slowly smiles.

> RICHARD
> It's about time.

The Captain looks unsure. Richard strides forward, the English clambering to get out of his way. He mounts a low rock and yells to the side.

> RICHARD
> Flanders. Come here.

FLANDERS steps out of another tent, a purple-clad Knight with a silvered longbow. Richard gestures at the castle.

RICHARD
A brave one. Worthy of your efforts.

Flanders smiles and walks over beside Richard. The Captain runs back and forth, cupping his hand around his mouth.

CAPTAIN
Cease fire. Cease fire.

The CRY is picked up and passed. Soon, no more arrows fly.

Richard grabs a banner and waves it a few times. The French Archer slowly raises the crossbow in a salute. Richard laughs and tosses the banner aside.

RICHARD
One shot, brave bowman. I'll not have it said I took advantage.

Flanders smiles cruelly and draws an arrow. The English back away, except for Richard and the Captain.

The French Archer watches.

Flanders slowly raises his bow, draws, hesitates. The English and French are still as stone. Flanders fires.

His arrow arches perfectly, climbing, silvery in the blue morning sky. The Troops hold their breath. The arrow bends gracefully toward the wall. The French Archer ignores it, watching Richard.

The arrow curves downward, its line true. Richard shakes his head slightly, almost looking sad, and lets out a faint sigh.

            RICHARD
  With a thousand such, I could march to China.

Flanders smirks. The French Archer slowly smiles. The arrow streaks down, straight at the Archer, straight at the Archer, straight . . .

EXT. ATOP FRENCH CASTLE WALL

. . . or curving slightly with the winds atop the wall. The arrow hisses by the Archer, scrapes an arm, and parts links in the chain mail. It THUNKS into the wooden platform behind.

EXT. OUTSIDE FRENCH CASTLE

Complete silence. Then PANDEMONIUM. French CHEERING, and mingled English GROANING, CHEERING, and severe head shaking.

After several seconds, the French Archer raises the crossbow. Sounds cut off like dousing a torch in a bucket.

The CLICKING of the ratchet can be heard as far away as Richard, as the Archer cocks the crossbow. A bolt is gently laid in the groove. The Archer raises the crossbow.

Flanders starts to creep away. Richard's arm shoots out and grabs him. Flanders' mouth twitches, but he catches the Captain's furious glance. He stays.

Richard spreads his arms and stares at the French Archer. The English grin and look up. The Archer aims.

The Archer fires.

The bolt jets downward. Flanders and the Captain stare at the arc, eyes going wide.

>RICHARD
>A brave shot, eh, men?

The bolt curves slightly with the breeze. Flanders and the Captain dive to the side.

>RICHARD
>In fact, an excellent—

Richard gapes momentarily. The bolt screams toward him. He starts to twist away.

>RICHARD
>Shit!

The bolt THUDS into his chest, near the heart. Richard collapses. The English Troops GASP. The Captain races up to cradle Richard's head. The French Archer watches from the battlements.

Richard waves the Troops back with one feeble hand. He stops when he has a clear view of the Archer.

>RICHARD
>A brave . . . shot.

He tries to salute the Archer.

RICHARD
If I had but a thousand . . . .

He sighs, eyes closing, and goes still. The Captain lets him down, muttering.

CAPTAIN
Bloody show-off.

EXT. ATOP FRENCH CASTLE WALL

The French Archer is helped down from the battlements. Some of the French offer congratulations. The Archer shrugs them off, and looks back down toward Richard.

Abruptly, the Archer reaches up and pulls off her helmet, revealing Marian. She turns and grabs the French Major.

MARIAN
You said something about a tunnel?

He nods sharply.

INT. DUNGEON CELL - DAY

John walks through the door, looks at Nottingham, and slowly shakes his head. Nottingham lets out a breath.

NOTTINGHAM
It was a long shot.

John glances out in the hall, then back at Nottingham.

JOHN
I was starting to look forward to helping foreigners.

NOTTINGHAM
If you ever get the chance, don't be obvious. If the people think you like outsiders, you'll spark another riot.

John frowns, then looks away a moment. His face clears.

JOHN
Act like I hate them, so I can help them?

NOTTINGHAM
Maybe. It's rather moot at the moment.

John nods sadly. He turns toward the door, then looks back.

JOHN
If they caught Marian, I'll be joining you soon. Keep the fires warm.

NOTTINGHAM
Where we're going, I don't think that's a problem.

John laughs and goes out, leaving the door open. A moment later, two BURLY PRISON GUARDS enter.

EXT. SHORE - DAY

Marian leaps out of a skiff and slogs through low surf to the muddy shore. A man rows the skiff back toward a ship, its single mast swaying back and forth.

MARIAN
(mumbling)
Useless boat. Stupid wind. Bloody mud. Damn sucking surf.

She makes it to dry land and dashes up a hill toward a dingy hovel. A horse stands saddled by the door.

EXT. JOHN'S CASTLE YARD - DAY

The two Burly Guards drag Nottingham into the sunlight, his hands chained in front of him. A SCAFFOLD stands near the door. More GUARDS line the path to it.

The CROWD surrounding the scaffold JEERS. More PEOPLE pour in through the main gate, including Robin and Tuck in wide-brimmed, floppy hats, trying to hide their faces. John Little follows.

Longchamp stands on the scaffold by a noose and sneers down at Nottingham. The Executioner wanders about, beaming pleasantly. He pushes a strange device higher up on his nose: two thick pieces of glass held over his eyes by poorly twisted wires.

Longchamp opens his arms to the Crowd.

LONGCHAMP
Presenting deceitful thief of taxes.

The Crowd THUNDERS its approval. The two Guards drag Nottingham. He throws them off. They come at him. He glares. They back off. He marches up the steps.

Longchamp back-pedals until the two Burly Guards join them on the scaffold.

> LONGCHAMP
> Hope you enjoyed wait. Told John waste time.

Nottingham marches over to the rope and stands by it. The Executioner pushes up his nose device and waves his fingertips at the Crowd.

Nottingham looks at John, seated on a special podium to the side with his PERSONAL GUARDS and Cogsworth. John raises his hands, palms up. Nottingham nods. Longchamp grabs the Executioner.

> LONGCHAMP
> Get on.

> EXECUTIONER
> Hmmm?

The Executioner looks around. His eyes slide over Nottingham, past Longchamp, and alight on the two Burly Guards. He strolls toward them, eyeing their bulk.

> EXECUTIONER
> Both at once? Rope ain't strong enough.

The Burly Guards look at each other and take a step back.

> LONGCHAMP
> Not them.

He grabs the Executioner and points him at Nottingham.

LONGCHAMP
Him.

The Guards look relieved. The Executioner studies Nottingham, walks partway around him, and looks back at Longchamp.

EXECUTIONER
He won't do at all. Oh, my, no.

Longchamp gapes. Nottingham raises an eyebrow.

EXECUTIONER
He's a noble.

Nottingham looks at John. John laughs. The Crowd MUTTERS and scratches random heads. Longchamp stares at the Executioner.

LONGCHAMP
Gravity works.

He gestures at the trap door. The Executioner removes his nose device and holds the glass disks up to the sun. He spits on one and rubs it with a shirttail.

EXECUTIONER
Can't happen.

LONGCHAMP
Could try.

EXECUTIONER
Won't work.

LONGCHAMP
Call it experiment.

The Executioner puts the device back on his nose, wires draped over his ears.

> EXECUTIONER
> Gotta behead nobles.

Longchamp's mouth opens and shuts. He glances around the scaffold—no block, no axe. He looks at the Executioner.

> LONGCHAMP
> Discrimination.

> EXECUTIONER
> It's allowed. It's the twelfth century.

> LONGCHAMP
> Almost thirteenth.

The Executioner jabs a thumb at the Guards.

> EXECUTIONER
> I could do one of those.

> LONGCHAMP
> No.

The Executioner shrugs and inspects the necks on the two Burly Guards. They twitch. Longchamp looks at them.

> LONGCHAMP
> Well? Why waiting? Fetch block.

The two Guards tumble over each other evacuating the scaffold.

LONGCHAMP
And axe. Hurry.

EXECUTIONER
Chop chop.

Longchamp gives the Executioner a dirty look. The Executioner grins. The two Guards race into the castle.

Longchamp glowers at John, who still chuckles. Longchamp spits at Nottingham's feet, storms off the scaffold, and follows the Guards. Nottingham looks at the sun.

EXT. FIELD - DAY

Globs of mud fly from the hooves of Marian's mare. She leans low over the horse's neck, digging in her heals.

MARIAN
All right, two studs. And candy apples. Dammit, move, you bloated bag of bony-headed god-forsaken . . .

EXT. JOHN'S CASTLE YARD - LATER

Nottingham looks at the sun. The Crowd pays no attention, arguing with VENDORS over the price of food.

Tuck grabs Robin before he comes to blows with a FRUIT VENDOR, and gives the Vendor a coin. The Vendor turns away. Robin pulls an apple from under his jerkin.

The Executioner stands beside Nottingham, fiddling with his nose device and pointing to people in the Crowd.

> EXECUTIONER
> . . . blonde, and black hair, and that one has blue eyes. My god, I can see eyes.

> NOTTINGHAM
> Take those off.

The Executioner looks confused, then points at his nose.

> EXECUTIONER
> Why—

> NOTTINGHAM
> It's 1199. Spectacles haven't been invented yet.

The Executioner slowly removes them, downcast.

> EXECUTIONER
> Oh. Right. Too bad, that.

He stuffs them in a pocket and peers sadly at his hands.

Longchamp bursts from the castle door carrying two axes, followed by the two Burly Guards lugging a headsman's block. The Crowd catches sight and CHEERS. Robin leans near Tuck.

> ROBIN
> About damn time.

John taps Cogsworth on the shoulder, at which Cogsworth leaves off arguing with the Fruit Vendor and waves his basket away.

Longchamp stalks up the scaffold steps and points to the far corner.

                    LONGCHAMP
        There.

The Guards stumble up the steps with the block and waddle toward the corner. Longchamp frowns at the bleary-eyed Executioner, who's trying to count his own fingers.

                    EXECUTIONER
        Four?

The Executioner pulls his hand closer and counts one set of fingers with the other. Only two were up.

                    EXECUTIONER
        Damn.

Longchamp thrusts out the two axes.

                    LONGCHAMP
        Which?

                    EXECUTIONER
        Which what?

The Executioner peers about. Longchamp shoves both axes into his hands. One is far too heavy, and the Executioner nearly takes off Longchamp's toe. Longchamp dances back.

LONGCHAMP
Watch it.

The Executioner lifts the other axe, holding it to his face and twisting it so the blade faces away.

EXECUTIONER
Wish I could. Damn calendar. Nothing's ever invented when you need it.

He hefts the blade and steps forward. Longchamp points at Nottingham, and the exhausted Guards lead him to the block. He kneels.

The Executioner swings the blade a few times and steps forward. He chops through one of the supports for the noose. The wooden frame topples onto the Crowd. The Fruit Vendor SCREAMS.

EXECUTIONER
Sorry. Didn't mean it.
    (mutters)
Who'd I hit? Skinny fellow.

Longchamp gets behind him and pushes him toward the block.

LONGCHAMP
There.

EXECUTIONER
What?

LONGCHAMP
Down. Prisoner.

> EXECUTIONER

Oh.

Longchamp straightens him and backs away. The Executioner turns.

> EXECUTIONER

Thank you very much. That was . . .

He tries to turn back, and peers around.

> EXECUTIONER

Oh, dear.

Longchamp rolls his eyes and steps up again, re-aiming him.

> EXECUTIONER

Yes, thank you. Most helpful.

Longchamp grabs his shoulders to keep him from turning again, then backs away and signals the Guards. They grab Nottingham's arms and hold his head to the block.

The Executioner keeps peering intently. He lifts the axe, tries to focus, adjusts his feet a little, raises the axe a tad more, and takes a deep breath, flexing his muscles. He tenses.

Marian bursts through the Crowd at the front gate.

> MARIAN

Richard has fallen! Shot in battle! Long live the King!

She points at John.

Nottingham jerks upright. The two Burly Guards, holding his arms, flop onto their backs. The Executioner CHOPS.

The Crowd follows Marian's eyes.

> CROWD
> Ahhhhh, crap.

John points. His personal Guards race toward the scaffold.

> LONGCHAMP
> Lie. Hold.

Longchamp's Guards, including Curly-Hair, engage John's. The Executioner dances from foot to foot.

Marian fights through the Crowd.

Nottingham knocks the two Burly Guards from the scaffold. Longchamp snatches a crossbow from another Guard.

> EXECUTIONER
> I hit it. I hit it.

The Executioner kneels and feels around the block.

Longchamp aims at John.

> LONGCHAMP
> Treason. Richard lives.

> EXECUTIONER
> Not much blood. I would've thought . . . .

Nottingham smashes his manacles onto Longchamp's crossbow. It fires. The bolt barely misses Cogsworth.

Longchamp trips Nottingham, then pulls a knife. He stabs. Nottingham deflects the blade with his cuffs.

Marian forces her mount closer.

John draws a sword. More of his Guards pour from the castle. Longchamp's forces pull back to defend the stairs of the scaffold. Curly-Hair is slain.

The Executioner wanders over to the noise. Nottingham gets up and swings at Longchamp. Longchamp stabs. They lurch. The knife sticks through a link of Nottingham's chain and gets buried in a crevice in a post. Nottingham is stuck.

Longchamp laughs and picks up the crossbow. He hammers his knife in further, then cocks the crossbow. Nottingham tugs on his chain, but the knife is tight. Longchamp aims at John.

Marian leaps from her horse and tackles Longchamp. His bolt just misses Cogsworth. Cogsworth lets out a long-suffering sigh.

Marian and Longchamp get up. She stalks him, leaps—and the Executioner stumbles and knocks her over. Longchamp laughs and grabs an axe. He stalks her back toward Nottingham.

Longchamp traps Marian in a corner. He swings.

Nottingham grabs the post and kicks the Executioner. The Executioner crashes into Longchamp and they plunge from the scaffold. The Executioner lands on top. Longchamp lands on the axe.

Marian pulls a pin from her hair and picks the lock on Nottingham's cuffs.

The Executioner sits up and clutches his head. He tries to waken Longchamp, but the Chancellor is cross-eyed and still.

> EXECUTIONER
> Oh, dear. Not again.

The last of Longchamp's Guards surrender.

Marian tears the cuffs from Nottingham's wrists. She attacks him, embracing him till his ribs crack. He yanks his arms from beneath her grasp and clutches her back.

John waves both hands at the Crowd. A few give token cheers.

> JOHN
> My first act shall be one of mercy. I grant Nottingham a pardon.

> ROBIN
> No!

Tuck muffles him. The rest of the Crowd MUTTERS like they sort of expected it. Marian and Nottingham kiss. Tuck drags Robin toward the gate. John Little goes out.

> JOHN
> And I grant the King's blessing to all foreigners.

The Crowd JEERS. John overrides them.

> JOHN
> If I give my peace even to a dog, that peace must be kept inviolate.

The Crowd MUMBLES over this. Several heads nod.

> OBESE GIANT
> I suppose that's fair.

> HATCHET-FACED WOMAN
> Dammit.

> JOHN
> And I'm cutting taxes in half.

Stunned silence. Then, finally, some real cheers. In a small knot, the Blue, Red, and Green Barons smile at each other.

> BLUE BARON
> Now we're talking.

> RED BARON
> He'll do.

> GREEN BARON
> Maybe.

The Blue and Red Barons beat the Green one with their hats. Robin stares at the turncoat Crowd.

> ROBIN
> Nooo . . . .

Nottingham and Marian keep kissing. John beams.

EXT. OUTSIDE CASTLE

Tuck hustles Robin out the main gate.

> TUCK
> Robin, it's time to retire.

> ROBIN
> But I lost all our—

> TUCK
> No, you didn't.

Robin give him a sidelong glance. Tuck grins and JINGLES a fat pouch. Robin gets his cocky look back. They saunter away.

> ROBIN
> So, where are we going?

> TUCK
> I was thinking Ireland.

> ROBIN
> We'll tell our adventures. We'll be famous.

Tuck chuckles and brandishes a quill.

> TUCK
> Naturally. History is in the pen of the beholder.

Robin grins and takes Tuck's arm, leaning against him. Tuck shakes him off, waving both hands. As they pass John Little, Robin leans near him.

> ROBIN
> Little John.

Tuck looks over, surprised. John Little's face goes red. Robin and Tuck take off, John Little in hot pursuit.

EXT. JOHN'S CASTLE YARD

On the scaffold, Marian and Nottingham break, gazing into each others' eyes.

>   MARIAN
> French scum.

>   NOTTINGHAM
> Trollop.

>   MARIAN
> To think I have to marry you.

>   NOTTINGHAM
> Good thing you called it off—

She stuffs his words with a kiss.

John waves to the cheering Crowd and smiles, almost smug. The Raven lands on a post behind him.

>   JOHN
> History will remember King John and the Sheriff of Nottingham.

He nods slowly. Cogsworth raises an eyebrow.

>   JOHN
> And Robin Hood and Richard will be known evermore for the villains they were.

RAVEN
Never.

John doesn't hear. He looks at Marian and Nottingham, and smiles.

JOHN
We're heroes.

RAVEN
More never. Nevermore.

The Raven swivels its head a couple of times.

RAVEN
That's it. Nevermore.

JOHN
Oh, shut up, Po.

Nottingham and Marian kiss. And Robin and Tuck disappear in the distance, John Little close behind, waving his quarterstaff.

FADE TO BLACK

THE END

Special Note:

Only one animal was injured in the making of this film. A parak . . . that is, canary, suffered a broken toenail. We apologized profusely, and the canary settled out of court for a sum we would rather not discuss.

Who'd've thought a raven made a good lawyer?

Of course, the entire population of England was accidentally slain in a botched special effect, but then, they're the ones who thought Richard was a good king. We imported a large quantity of penguins to replace them, and no one seems to have noticed.

Historical Notes:

This tale crams in more historical accuracy than any other Robin Hood story you've seen, thus proving beyond a doubt that this is the one true version of how it really happened. And if you don't believe me, tough pomegranates.

a) When the three whores play like Shakespearean witches and tell Richard to beware March 26th, that's the day he was shot. And yes, Richard did team up with Philip of France to fight Henry II, so it was patricide.

b) There is a legend that when Richard first entered the room of his dead father, a bit of blood spurted from Henry's mouth. Of course, no one pumped his finger to get it out.

c) Under Henry, Jews were tolerated in England, but riots broke out after Richard took the throne. John forced tolerance again when he took power, and his line "If I give my peace even to a dog, that peace must be kept inviolate" is a direct quote. He's called anti-Semitic for saying it, but look at the result.

d) The amount of Richard's ransom (when he was caught by Germans on his way home from the crusades) is exact. The inflation factor is getting worse all the time.

e) The location and show-off manner of Richard's death is actually how it happened. OK, he might have been shot by a French crossbowman instead of by Marian, and he lingered a few days before dying, but where's the drama in that?

f) Longchamp didn't get killed immediately. In reality, he dressed up in women's clothes and tried to sneak out of England. He was caught in a small boat at the coast by John's men. If it weren't anticlimactic, that could have been funny. Well, not to Longchamp . . . .

(Oh—and apologies to those great tales I poked a little fun at. Recognize them?)

THE WICKED WITCH OF THE YEAST

Oblique serrated teeth aside,
Discounting her relentless pride,
Or pupils hard as mountainside,
There's no witch quite like Scone.
She tends to savor guts and gore
And has a vice you might deplore—
She'd gladly burn you to the core
And relish every moan.

Her specialty is making bread
By molding dough around the head
Until her victim waxes dead.
Her loaves have quite a taste.
She kneads the paste before she starts,
Then finds her favorite victims: tarts,
Attractive ones with little smarts.
Unchaste, disgraced, debased.

She went to Clyde-on-Avon once
And thought she'd found the perfect dunce,
A dockside harlot serving punts,
So Scone got out her yeast.
She left her dough to rise. With guile
Tricked the wench, a lie most vile,
Followed by a twisted smile.
"Come, we'll have a feast."

But Scone had made a small mistake.
The boating whore was just a fake:
Cop Dee le Ven, sent there to make
Old Scone regret her kicks.
The cop resisted all Scone's spells:
Missiles, darts, outrageous smells,
Flashing lights from Dante's hells—
Le Ven knew all her tricks.

The cop tied Scone and took her flour;
Dipped and cooked her for an hour.
This ablution failed. Sour
Scone stayed full corrupt.
So brave le Ven took yeast in hand
And stuffed the witch with fungus bland.
Le Ven hoped Scone could not withstand
The gas that would erupt.

But though she left Scone in the sun
And thought her task for certain done,
The yeasty work had just begun
When evil Scone escaped.
The witch regurgitated all,
Burned off her bonds and left a scrawl:
With bold, unmitigated gall,
Insulted, taunted, japed.

Le Ven continues searching still.
No rest while Scone is free. Her skill
Must seek the wicked witch until
The hag is but a ghost.
So if someday you meet a crone
With hollow loaf and eyes of stone,
And if that biddy's name is Scone—
Beware, or you'll be toast.

The Yend

FADE IN:

EXT. MOUNTAIN PATH - DAY

Four HIKERS tote packs up a trail below a ridge. Rock rises to one side and a sheer drop brackets them on the other.

They round a bend and see a rock fall blocking the path twenty feet ahead. They trudge toward it slowly, then stop a few feet away.

> JIMMY
Oh, man.

SHARON slumps, looking back the way they came. GEORGE shrugs, drops his pack, and pulls out a sandwich. PATTY just raises an eyebrow.

> PATTY
Come on, out of the way. No big deal.

The others look confused as Patty shoos them back down the path and around the curve, out of sight. She turns back to the blockage, plunks down her pack, and pulls out a notebook computer.

She also pulls out a camera, trailing a wire which she plugs into the notebook. She kneels, pokes a few keys, then aims the camera at the trail and clicks.

On the computer screen, a picture of the trail appears. Patty grabs a light pen and strokes the screen as if with a paint brush. She paints out the rocks blocking the path, touches up the trail, and pauses.

> SHARON (O.S.)
> Wish *I'd* brought a sandwich.

> JIMMY (O.S.)
> Long time till supper if we gotta backtrack.

> GEORGE (O.S.)
> Anyone got mustard?

Patty looks over her shoulder at the curve in the trail. She grins, turns back to the screen, and paints bright red dots on a small bush where the blockage used to be. She hits a key and the earth TREMBLES.

SCREECHES and SCRAPES abound as the other three hikers fall to the ground.

Patty dusts herself off and stows her equipment while the others stumble into view.

> JIMMY
> Holy shmoley . . .

> SHARON
> Cripes, look at that.

Ahead, the trail is open, matching the picture Patty modified on the computer. George races ahead and plucks red berries off the bush.

> GEORGE
> I'm looking, I'm looking.

He stuffs his face, staring at the berries. The others walk past up the trail, Jimmy and Sharon in shock, Patty looking pleased with herself. George belatedly follows.

NARRATOR (V.O.)
Macrohard—the leading edge in artistic expression.

FADE TO BLACK

CUPID'S REVENGE

FADE IN:

EXT. STREET - NIGHT

A YOUNG WOMAN stops at a mailbox and opens it. Her eye catches a waxing half moon high in the sky. She pauses to admire it. The lower corner of the moon disappears.

Another car pulls into the driveway next door and a MAN gets out.

>   MAN
> What's up?

The young woman points at the moon. More of the lower point disappears.

>   YOUNG WOMAN
> I love eclipses.

A neighbor LADY wanders over, looking up.

>   LADY
> Eclipsi. Like octopi.

>   MAN
> Then it would be eclippi. But it's not eclippus, so—

>   YOUNG WOMAN
> Would you two freeze it?

The man and lady glare at the young woman, then look at each other, bat eyes, and move closer together. They gaze at the moon. The lower third is cut off by a curving shadow.

Another car pulls up. The lights shut off. An old PROFESSOR gets out.

> YOUNG WOMAN
> Look, an eclipse.

The professor stomps over to the others, not looking up.

> PROFESSOR
> What are you talking about? It's a half moon.

> MAN
> So?

> PROFESSOR
> The earth can't be in the sun's way unless it's a full moon.

> LADY
> Why not?

> YOUNG WOMAN
> Oh, I see. The moon has to be *opposite* the sun.

The professor nods.

> MAN
> Then what's blocking the moon?

The professor goes blank-faced. The young woman blinks at the professor. The lady and man move apart.

The professor turns and they all look up. The half-moon is over half gone.

EXT. SURFACE OF MOON

A chubby little CUPID mutters to himself, flying along just above the surface with his bow and quiver slung across his back. A couple of hearts dangle from the bottom of his quiver.

In one hand Cupid carries a can of black paint. A plastic hose trails up to his other hand, where he wields a spray gun. The moon turns black as he flutters past.

>   CUPID
> Four thousand years and not a single friggin' vacation. Damn lovers. All the moon's fault. Fix them. No moon, no love, no more damn Cupid arrows. Going fishing. That's what I'll do. And golf. If I ever figure what that stupid game is all about . . . .

He sprays on and on. The moon fades away behind him.

FADE TO BLACK

MACROHARD #3

FADE IN:

INT. DEN - DAY

A WOMAN lifts the cover off a computer. She snaps in a card, pulls over a cable, and plugs it into the card. She lowers the cover.

The Woman sits before the reassembled computer, the screen glowing with an address list. She scans up the list, bottom to top. Names flow past, each highlighted in turn.

She pauses at SATAN, her eyes going a bit wide.

She pans further back, noting THE POPE, and snorting when GOD appears. She reaches CTHULHU and stops, looking slightly puzzled.

> WOMAN
> Cthulhu? The call of . . . . H. P. Lovecraft?

She shrugs and hits return. BEEPS sound as the connection goes through. A loud HISSING follows, then CREAKING and crashing SURF.

Her computer shivers. She looks alarmed. A hideous HOWLING and CRASHING follow, as the computer shudders and rocks.

She jabs escape several times to no avail, then leaps back as the top blows off the monitor. She looks over her shoulder.

                    WOMAN
          Diane, I think I—

The remainder of the monitor explodes and the
computer ruptures open. Inside, a broiling, churning
mass of colors spins and distorts. Massive, slimy
green tentacles burst out and grip the sides of the
desk.

The Woman races SCREAMING from the room. A
tentacle whips out the door, snatches her leg, and
drags her back in.

                    NARRATOR (V.O.)
          Macrohard—the leading edge in on-line
          communications.

FADE TO BLACK

BURIAL

FADE IN:

EXT. CEMETERY - NIGHT

A panel truck pulls up inside an ancient cemetery, near a decrepit old church. The side of the truck reads, "MIDNIGHT INTERMENT—SATISFACTION LIKELY."

MOURNERS pile out and gather around an old gravestone. No one else is visible.

An air compressor in the truck POUNDS to life. The FUNERAL DIRECTOR walks from the truck carrying a ten-foot long, slender rod. A three-way valve at one end of the rod is attached to a hose which trails back to the truck.

> DIRECTOR
> And this environmentally correct procedure avoids the waste of precious land.

The mourners look uneasy. The Director jams the rod six feet into the ground just in front of the gravestone. He presses a button. The rod vibrates and goes a bit deeper.

He gets a jug from the truck and walks back, waving the jug at the Mourners.

> DIRECTOR
> Yes, folks, this biodegradable slurry of cremation ash and common ethyl alcohol will soak poor old Alfred right into—

He peers at the gravestone a moment.

> DIRECTOR
> —Miss Templeton's long-dried bones. A quality grave site for a pittance, if I do say so myself.

The Mourners grimace as he fastens the jug to the valve atop the rod.

From behind a tree, a PREACHER looks on. He blinks, looking confused.

A SUCKING comes from the Director's jug. The mourners fidget.

> DIRECTOR
> Dear Lord, we ask that you welcome Alfred, even if he can't afford his own hole.

A mourning OLD WOMAN WAILS, clutching a handkerchief.

> DIRECTOR
> After all, Lord, it's the century of recycling, and, well, we figure you'll understand.

Behind his tree, the Preacher looks horrified.

> PREACHER
> Desecration!

The sucking stops and the Director disconnects the jug.

> DIRECTOR
> OK, folks. He's in the bosom of the Lord now. Or at least in Miss Templeton's bosom.

The Old Woman wails again. Two other Mourners lead her back to the truck. The Director pulls his rod from the ground.

The Preacher stares, stunned.

> PREACHER
> Heresy.

EXT. CEMETERY - ANOTHER NIGHT

The panel truck parks amidst old headstones. The Funeral Director gets out with his rod, and follows a few MOURNERS toward an old grave.

The Preacher tops off a jug from a water tap outside the church. The jug looks just like the kind the Director uses. The Preacher sneaks toward the panel truck.

An OLD MAN leads the Mourners to one stone.

> OLD MAN
> What can we say about poor old Fitzgibbons? His death was shocking.

The other Mourners look at him strangely.

> OLD MAN
> Well, they electrocuted him, didn't they?

> DIRECTOR
> Then you've picked an excellent grave, my friends. This was a confidante of Edison.

The Mourners look at him.

DIRECTOR
A confederate, then. Look . . .

He points at the gravestone.

DIRECTOR
. . . they lived about the same time. More or less.

The Mourners look at each other. The Director jabs his rod deep into the grave and heads for the truck.

The Preacher switches jugs and darts out of sight just as the Director reaches in. The Director grabs the new jug, starts the compressor motor, goes back to the grave, and connects the jug to the rod.

OLD MAN
So long, Fitzgibbons. Rest in pieces.

They all watch the jug. A SUCKING noise gurgles from it.

A light comes on in the church. The Mourners panic and pile into the truck. The Director yanks the rod from the ground, water spraying from the end. A WOMAN MOURNER gasps. The Director tosses the equipment in the truck.

DIRECTOR
Don't worry, ma'am. He's pretty much all in the hole.

He hurries them all in and they take off.

The Preacher walks onto the grave site from the direction of the church, carrying the jug he stole. He shakes his fist at the truck.

PREACHER
Sacrilege.

He caresses the jug with his free hand. Looks around. No one is visible. He uncorks the jug and drinks. He gags and makes a face, then waves the jug toward the truck.

PREACHER
How dare they waste good alcohol.

He shakes his head as the truck disappears in the distance.

PREACHER
'Course, might taste better if I filter it.

He shrugs and takes another swallow.

FADE TO BLACK

SENTIENT CHOICE

"ALL RISE. THE Department of Revenue of the State of Illinois versus Unit A-Seventeen-Q-Z-Forty. The Honorable Judge Wendy Treadmoore presiding."

"Objection."

Judge Treadmoore paused in the act of sitting down and looked at the defendant. "Objection to what? We haven't started yet."

Unit A17QZ40 leaned his hands on the massive oak table as if his legs would soon betray him. A ripple of humid August breeze barely stirred his thick black hair; the air conditioning was out again. He wrinkled his nose at the scent of rot off the heavy brown river outside. "Your Honor, a tax court does not have jurisdiction to determine so significant a matter as the legal status of robots. In fact, the legitimacy of using a trial for any piece of machinery has not been established."

The judge snorted and resumed the process of settling her bulk into the overstuffed chair behind the bench. She picked up her gavel and rapped it once. "Case open. Overruled. This is a matter of earnings, and whether the state has a right to an appropriate share."

The three-foot-six bailiff took a deep breath and turned toward the courtroom.

"Everybody sit down," said Judge Treadmoore.

"Be . . . seated," said the bailiff, pouting at the judge.

"Your Honor," said a gaunt man, hopping to his feet before his bottom could more than graze the chair behind him.

"Yes? Williams, isn't it?"

"Andersen, Your Honor. Jonathan Andersen. I was in your court yesterday."

"Oh, right. What do you want?"

"As prosecutor, I move for a summary judgment in favor of the state. I mean, look at him. He's sweating, nervous, foolish enough to try representing himself—in short, he exhibits all the traits of real humans in court. He is obviously a 'person' and, as such, owes appropriate taxes on everything he's earned since he was manufactured three years ago. Plus penalties and interest for failure to file in past years."

"Williams—"

"Andersen, Your Honor."

"—you can't get a summary conviction. Not even in tax court. Only summary dismissal if the case is hypered. Do you want me to conclude you've researched this case as badly as yesterday's?"

"No, Your Honor."

"Then sit down and shut up."

"Yes, ma'am."

"'Your Honor.'"

"Sorry, Your Honor."

"How long have you been out of law school?"

"Your Honor?"

"Never mind. You can stand up again and open your case now."

"Oh. Right. Thank you." Andersen took a deep breath and turned toward the empty jury box; he quickly redirected his attention to the judge. "Your honor, we will show that Unit A17QZ40 has in fact all the valid traits necessary to qualify for classification as a person, and that as such all his earnings should be taxed at the same rate as for human citizens, rather than the greatly lesser rate for manufacturing processes."

He stopped when the judge waved a finger.

"Ma'am?"

"Wrong."

"Sorry. Your Honor had a question?"

"Yes. How can anything be 'greatly lesser?'"

Andersen stared at her in confusion.

"Never mind," said the judge. "I wouldn't want to overtax you."

Andersen chuckled. "Overtax. That's a . . . I mean, this being . . . sorry. I'll just continue then, shall I?"

Judge Treadmoore closed her eyes and nodded.

Andersen smiled tentatively, then dropped it. "As I said, Unit A17QZ40 should be taxed as a human, not a machine conducting a manufacturing process. This would result in a difference of four point six three percent of his earnings over the past year, for the State of Illinois alone, and more for the federal government and the various states through which he has been eluding us."

"Objection," said Unit A17QZ40.

"Sustained. Stick to relevant details. You're not trying to prove willful neglect or evasion, I thought."

Andersen wiped his forehead. "No, Your Honor. You told us that would be politically too sensitive."

"Objection. Move for dismissal. Your Honor, you advised the prosecution?"

"Sit down, robot," said Treadmoore. "This is tax court, not criminal law. Carry on, Mister Prosecutor."

"Yes. Anyway, the total the state seeks to collect, considering extensive book and movie royalties as well as speaking engagements, is approximately fifty-five point two million dollars."

"Obje—"

"Oh, shut up."

Andersen hesitated, but the judge didn't add anything, so he raced on. "Considering the earnings of all the other robots of A17QZ40's type and later designs, the state stands to recoup in excess of three hundred seventy million dollars by classifying them as sentient persons. And far more in the future. For our first witness we call Amanda Gooligan."

"Amanda Gooligan," intoned the bailiff, scanning the courtroom. "Amanda Gooligan, please."

"She's right behind you," said Judge Treadmoore.

"She . . ."

"And quite a bit above you."

The bailiff glanced up at Amanda and the judge. "They're supposed to come up the center aisle."

"Well, don't worry about it. Just swear her in."

He muttered something and accomplished the task, glaring at the prim blonde woman until she had recited her name, address, age, marital status (single), and favorite ice cream.

"Bailiff!"

He smirked at the judge and withdrew.

Andersen swaggered over to the witness stand and laid one hand on the railing. "Miss Gooligan—"

"Ms."

"I beg your . . . oh, of course. Ms. Gooligan, what is your relationship with the defendant."

"I made him what he is today."

Judge Treadmoore sighed. "Please, Ms. Gooligan."

"Sorry. I made him."

"Meaning," asked the prosecutor, "you physically manufactured Unit A17QZ40?"

"No, of course not. A whole plant worked on that. I headed the design group that created Asev, and

I oversaw the manufacture, QC, and testing before we cleared him for delivery."

"QC?" asked the judge.

"Quality control."

"Very well," said Andersen. "And after 'Asev' was delivered, what was your relationship with him."

"Objection," said Unit A17QZ40. "The use of the term 'him' implies the status of a person, which we have not yet established. I am an 'it.'"

"You've got a—" said Amanda, turning red as she looked at the judge and shrank back in her chair.

Judge Treadmoore looked from the witness to the defendant to the court reporter. "Strike that last comment from the record." The court reporter furiously scratched something on his note pad, while the judge furrowed her brows. "What happened to the computer records? And who are you, anyway?"

"I. Am. Unit. 6BM71. Your. Honor. The. Computer. Is. Broken. I. Take. Shorthand. The. Human. Court. Reporter. Was. Unable. To. Do. So."

Judge Treadmoore stared a moment longer, blinked a few times, then looked back at the defendant. "You dress in the classic style of a male, and I'm sure I've seen numerous references in the press which used the term 'he' over the years, to which you've never objected. It's a bit late now. Overruled." She paused. "'Asev?'"

"That was purely a convenient shortening of A17QZ40, not a sign of person status." Asev rubbed his hands on his pants and glanced around the courtroom for support. There wasn't a lot. Mostly others waiting their turn in the dock, amused at his plight. If the state won the case against him, maybe the judge would be in a more charitable mood for them. "Lots of machines are referred to by abbreviations," he said limply.

"Very well. Continue, Williams."

"Ander, uh, sen," said the prosecutor. "I believe you were going to describe your relationship with the defendant, Ms. Gooligan?"

"I was his lover for eleven months."

"Really?" Judge Treadmoore leaned forward and looked down at the witness. "Was he any good?"

"Objection." said Asev.

"Your Honor," said Andersen, "please let me ask the questions."

"Were you going to ask that one?"

"Er, no."

"Well, then."

Andersen's shoulders slumped. "Ms. Gooligan, was he any good?"

"Objection!"

"Oh, all right, never mind," said the judge. "Sustained."

"Actually, yes," said Amanda, ignoring the ruling. "But he got tired too easily."

"Well, it was your own faulty design, then," said Treadmoore.

"Your Honor!" said the prosecutor.

"Sorry, Williams. Carry on."

"Er . . . sen. Um. Ms. Gooligan, can you describe Asev's development since manufacture?"

"Yes."

". . . Well?"

"You wish me to? Very well. He began as an educated baby, full of encyclopedic knowledge and physically an adult, but with no motor coordination and no mental acuity. These developed rapidly, of course, as they do in less advanced models as well, since development of the auto-hume cortico-simulator."

Andersen raised a hand. "An auto court . . ."

Gooligan smiled. "Close enough. By four months he could move and converse like the best of the non-sentient robots."

"Objection," said Asev. "The point of this trial is to establish whether or not I am sentient, and hence a person. Amanda's . . . Ms. Gooligan's statement implies—"

"Sustained. Please stick to the facts, Ms. Gooligan."

"Hmph," said Amanda. "I mean, sorry, Your Honor."

Andersen's knuckles whitened on the railing. "May we continue?"

"Sure," said Judge Treadmoore. "Amanda, when did you first sleep with him?"

"Your Honor!" said Andersen.

"Get on with it yourself, then."

The prosecutor's body began twitching. "Ms. Gooligan, at what point did you first suspect Asev had become sentient?"

"Objection. Council is leading the—"

"Yes, yes, we know all that, Asev," said the judge. "But she's a prosecution witness; obviously she thinks you're sentient. Let's just get on with it. Answer the question, Amanda."

"Well, I had my thoughts for several months. But you see, as the designer I was afraid my judgment might be biased. I might be seeing something I wanted, that wasn't really there. You understand?"

"Certainly," said the judge.

"Certainly," said the prosecutor, glaring at the judge.

"Certainly," said the bailiff, smiling when everyone turned to glare at him.

"Anyway," said Amanda, "I thought he was sentient before we became lovers, of course. But I became convinced he was fully aware and conscious, just like a human, when he began cheating on me."

"He what?" said Treadmoore.

Andersen pointed a quivering finger at the judge. "Please!"

"Just like a man," said Amanda, sniffling and looking at the defendant. "And not just once. Lots of times. And he had no taste. Some of them . . . . Well, never mind. Anyway, he also drank too much, though I understand he stopped that after I threw him out."

"Objection," said Asev.

"On what grounds?" asked Treadmoore.

Asev paused. "Hearsay?"

"What, that you drank, or that you quit?"

"I'm not sure, Your Honor."

"Let me know when you figure it out. You should have gotten a lawyer. Continue, Amanda."

"That's about all, I guess," said Gooligan. "I mean, he stopped playing chess with me when I couldn't give him a good game anymore, but I suppose any machine would do that. And he's got a weird sense of humor—he subscribes to *Poor Taste Games Quarterly*—but I don't know as that makes him a person."

"Thank you very much," said Andersen, staring at the judge's open mouth, daring her to ask something else. The mouth shut. "Your witness," he said to the defendant.

Asev looked from Andersen to Gooligan. "No, she's not. She's your witness."

Andersen rolled his eyes. "Don't try the literal game. You read mysteries. You know what the expression means."

Asev licked his lips and stood up. "Ms. Gooligan . . ."

"I'm still Amanda, aren't I?"

Asev chewed his lip a couple of times, then looked down at his notes. "Before I left you, I believe I explained I was conducting research on the differing physical stimuli associated with a variety of female—"

"Ha!" said Judge Treadmoore.

"Your Honor? I beg your pardon?" said Asev.

"Do you know how many men have tried that line? Variety, indeed."

"Thank you," said Amanda. "I couldn't have said it better myself. And you didn't leave me, Asev. I threw you out."

"You . . . never mind." Asev coughed and shuffled to another page of notes.

"And another thing," said Amanda. "What's so scientific about making me get silk sheets, and wear those kinky—"

"That will be all," said Asev, abruptly sitting down. "No further questions."

"Yes," said the prosecutor, rising. "What about—"

"Can it," said the judge. "We got the point, and we have a lot of ground to cover. Call your next witness."

The morning ground on as one witness after another gave examples of Asev's spontaneous generosity, sudden passions for ballet and astronomy, disdain of televangelists . . . . Asev drummed his fingers on the table and doodled on his pad, but seldom found a decent question to challenge the testimony. Then a priest took the stand and commended his repair of a broken organ.

"There," he yelped, jumping to his feet. "And after I fixed it, what did you do?"

The priest raised an eyebrow. "I tried to convert you, of course."

"Of course. And my response?"

"You said you didn't believe in God, or in any established religion for that matter."

"There. See, Your Honor? Doesn't that prove I'm deficient in a key aspect of humanity? I can't be truly sentient if I don't believe in God."

Judge Treadmoore let a smile play about her lips. "I certainly hope it doesn't prove that," she said. "I happen to be a rationalist, myself."

"Actually," said the priest, "you demonstrated remarkable tolerance for the beliefs of others. I thought you not merely a person when you left, but in fact an unusually kind one. I'm sorry this is going to cost you a little money, but isn't that worth the acknowledgment—"

"A little? A *little!* Do you have any idea how much they want? I've already spent it. They'll send me to jail. I can't *afford* to be a person."

"Bailiff," snapped the judge.

"Yes, what seems to be the problem?" The bailiff kicked his chair back and leaned against the wall. "Seems like perfectly normal courtroom decorum, don't you think?"

Asev threw up his hands and sat down. The priest apparently decided they were through with him, so he got up and left. Andersen put his head on the table.

"How much longer is this going to be?" said Amanda from the audience. "I have an appointment at noon."

Judge Treadmoore rapped her gavel. "I'm sure you may leave at any time. Wake up, Williams. Are you through, yet?"

Andersen unfolded his body and stood up. "The revenuers rest." He sat down and put his head back on his arms. The bailiff chuckled.

"Mr. Asev?" said the judge.

"Just 'Asev.' No 'mister.'"

"*Mister* Asev, do you have any witnesses to call?"

He rose and peered around. "Just one, I'm afraid. Ms. Collingsford from the American Civil Liberties Union."

"Collingsford, ACLU," called the bailiff from his position against the wall. "Front and center."

A pole-shaped woman with thick glasses and traces of a mustache stumbled forward to stand beside Asev. "I'm terribly sorry, sir. My boss has overruled me."

"What?" Asev stepped back, looking as if he were about to cry. "But you promised. I did everything you said. I got rid of my stamp collection, and model railroad . . . ." He wound down, glancing at the judge.

"But sir," said Ms. Collingsford, "as my boss rightly pointed out, either you're not a person and we shouldn't be helping you, or you are, so we shouldn't be helping you. It doesn't leave us much choice."

"Er," said Asev. "I don't suppose I could get my stamps back? I may need them to pay off—"

"I'm sorry," said Collingsford. "We already sold them to pay some bills. We're not a rich organization, you know."

"Yes. Well. Thanks anyway. At least you tried."

The woman stepped forward and patted his arm. "You're a nice man. I do hope you win your case."

She turned and left. Asev merely sank into his seat.

"Well." The judge grinned wickedly. "Well, well." She looked from Asev to the prosecutor. "Do either of you have anything more to contribute before I make my judgment in this case?"

Andersen looked up, then stood briefly. "I think it's quite clear. I don't see how I can lose this one."

"I don't either." The judge smirked. "But if anyone could have . . ."

"Thanks," mumbled Andersen, sitting down.

"And you?" said Treadmoore, gazing at Asev.

A17QZ40 stood and leaned on the oak table again. He stared down for a few moments, then looked out the window at the swollen river. Swollen, massive, as if a dam had . . . .

His eyes opened wide.

"Voting," he whispered. Then again, louder, looking at the judge. "Voting. You wouldn't want robots to be voting citizens, would you? If you make us people, you're opening the floodgates, breaking the dam. Before long, they'll be treating us like everyone else, with laws to protect our rights. Would you want your daughter marrying a robot?" His eyes glowed. He had them. Glorious, reliable prejudice would rear its sorry skull. The nervous shuffling in the audience confirmed his hopes.

Then Judge Treadmoore spoke.

"I don't believe in slippery slope arguments. It took years for equitability to fully manifest in civil rights cases. Who knows, for your kind? Anyway, we are not here to determine the status of your citizenship; that doesn't affect taxes. We're here to determine whether you and your compatriots can continue to fleece the taxpayers' coffers of their fair due by clinging to a machine status that clearly no longer applies. Three hundred seventy million dollars to date, and more every year. Did you really think we'd let you get away with that?

"No," she continued. "I'm afraid the evidence is clear, and we really have no choice. I find you, Asev, or A17QZ40, and every artificial intelligence of equal or greater capability, to be a person, and subject to the rights and privileges of full taxpayer status. You have ten days to present me with a plan, agreed with by your local Internal Revenue Service office, for the payment of all appropriate back taxes and interest. I will waive penalties for the sake of fairness.

"Case closed. Court will resume in two hours, after lunch."

"All rise for lunch," said the bailiff, still leaning against the wall. On her way out the door, the judge emptied her water glass over his head.

The court reporter hurried over to catch the prosecutor before he left. "Sir?" he asked. "Can. I. Get. The. Spelling. On. Your. Name. Is. That. Williamsen. With. An. E. N. Or. O. N?"

Andersen sniffed and walked away.

Outside tax court, automated news trucks mobbed Asev, and their human counterparts were worse. All wanted a seven-second sound bite regarding his victory for robot rights. Beyond were a smattering of robots and people—no, that was robots and *other* people—cheering him and waiving finger V's. He struggled past, while they congratulated his bravery, his clever ploy on behalf of computer sentience. He smiled feebly, waved, and snuck away as soon as he could.

Back in his apartment, Asev poured himself a stiff whiskey and collapsed on the sofa in the living room. He turned on the viewer and jumbled through stations until he found some old Bugs Bunny cartoons. After a moment, he picked up the thermostat remote and turned the air conditioning way high.

Then he pulled out his checkbook and contemplated it. But the answer wasn't there. So he turned on his computer system and called up blueprints for the city sewer system, the electrical wiring diagram for the downtown region, the floor plans for the basement of the First Fidelity Trust Bank, and the ordering specifications for silenced drills and power cutters. He pondered the printouts.

After a time, he sighed and crumpled up the documents. He was throwing them out when the phone rang.

"Hello?"

"Oh, Asev, I just heard. Congratulations."

"Mrs. Rothmorton, I've missed you. Er, thanks. And, um, happy seventy-fifth."

"Now Asev, I told you not to remind a woman of her age."

"Sorry. You're right. I'm kind of overloaded right now."

"Well, that's understandable. I wanted to let you know I've been talking with Melissa Argamonk and some of the others."

"You know Melissa?"

"Oh, don't be naive. I know you get around."

"Yes, ma'am. You know about Candice, then, too?"

"You . . . slept with my granddaughter?"

"She *is* twenty-nine," said Asev. "She heard of me from you."

"Ah. Well, never mind. Anyway, you should know we've collected almost fifteen million dollars already, and more is pouring in. Even some of the more frugal robots are helping out. We'll get you all off the hook."

Asev stared at the phone.

"Asev?"

"I . . . thank you, Mrs. Rothmorton. You don't know what this means."

"Oh, I think I do. Come around and visit me sometime, why don't you."

"I will. Thanks again. For all of us. And please say hello to your mother for me."

There came a pause. Followed by a thin, pale squeak.

"My *mother?*"

MACROHARD #7

FADE IN:

INT. KID'S BEDROOM - DAY

JENNIFER yanks a joystick back and forth in front of a computer. Lights FLASH. DINKS and BOINKS punctuate her motions. The room around the teenage girl is piled with dirty clothes and scattered books and papers.

Her MOTHER enters. Jennifer jabs a key and the screen flashes to a page of text; she ditches the joystick.

> MOTHER
> That wasn't homework.

> JENNIFER
> (sarcastic)
> What? I'm doing my paper.

The Mother glares, glances around, makes a face, and goes out. Behind her, DINKS and BOINKS resume.

INT. LIVING ROOM

The Mother walks in as ROB saunters by, jeans slung low on his lanky teenaged hips. Rob munches on a huge sandwich. He offers it to CONNIE, another teen in motorcycle black leather lounging in the front door. Connie shakes her head and tosses ROB a helmet.

                    CONNIE
          Let's go, deuce.

                    ROB
          That's "ace," baby.

Connie snorts.

                    MOTHER
          And what about *your* homework?

                    ROB
          It'll get done.

Connie grins at him and they go out.

The Mother stares at the door a moment, then strides
to another computer in the corner of the room. She
yanks a box off the shelf, rips off cellophane, pulls
out a disk, and shoves it in the CD tray. She clicks a
mouse a couple of times.

                    MOTHER
          Standard features?

She shrugs and hits a key. A loud BRAP erupts from
the computer's speaker. The Mother flinches. She
covers her ears and shakes her head. Three narrow
beams of red laser light shoot from the monitor to
the walls, in the directions of the three teenagers. A
second later, Jennifer sticks her head into the room.

                    JENNIFER
          Mom? I finished the paper. Want me to run
          laundry after I clean up?

The Mother nods dumbly and Jennifer disappears. The front door bursts open. Rob and Connie lean in.

> ROB
> Mom? Change of plans. We're going to the library for biology. See you at six.

They disappear before the Mother can react. She swivels from the door to the computer screen, then stares at a manual she lifts from the CD box. It falls open in her hand.

> MOTHER
> Advanced features. Boyfriends and girlfriends.

She looks thoughtfully toward the front door.

> NARRATOR (V.O.)
> Macrohard—the leading edge in behavioral psychology.

FADE TO BLACK

THE DEMISE OF SOCKS

FADE IN:

INT. BEDROOM - DAY

A WOMAN in a sweatsuit yanks off her socks, wipes perspiration from her brow, and tosses the socks in a laundry basket.

INT. BEDROOM - LATER

A MAN hefts the laundry basket.

> WOMAN
> Try not to lose any this time.

> MAN
> I wish I knew where they went.

The Man trudges from the room.

INT. LAUNDRY ROOM

The Man empties the basket into a washing machine, slams the lid, and punches a couple of buttons. He leaves. The machine HISSES as water pours in.

INT. LAUNDRY ROOM - LATER

The machine RUMBLES, QUAKES, and SNORTS. It goes silent, then HUMS into the drain cycle.

The dials begin to glow, distorting and turning into eyes and bushy brows. The eyebrows twitch upwards twice. The eyes look down.

INT. WASHING MACHINE

The water spins, slowly draining. Suddenly, two arms grow from the central spinner. Hands appear. As the clothes whirl past, they dive into the water and come up with a sock.

The machine QUAKES with a distant CHUCKLE, and the hands twist the sock into an impossibly narrow straw. They reach down and stuff the sock into a drain hole. The sock disappears with the water.

INT. PIPES

The sock flows through pipe after pipe.

EXT. CITY - DAY

An overhead image of suburbia whips past—streets, stores, and a distant sewage plant.

INT. PIPES

The sock whisks along.

EXT. CITY

The image races to the sewage plant, spins around an outdoor settling pool several times, then takes off toward a river.

INT. PIPES

The sock sails around bends and joints. Suddenly, it washes out the end of a pipe into a river.

EXT. RIVER

The overhead image flies down the river to the sea. Muddy river water spreads out, invading the blue of the ocean. The view dives into the water.

EXT. UNDER WATER

A MERMAID holds her nose as a spurt of brownish water dilutes itself in front of her. She frowns, peering at the sock as it settles to the sand. She picks it up.

She studies it, stretches it between her hands, then flips up her tail and glances from the tip to the sock. She scratches her head.

The Mermaid tosses the sock over her shoulder and swims away. The sock lands in a pile of a thousand others.

                    ANNOUNCER (V.O.)
          Now you know.

FADE TO BLACK

MACROHARD #5

FADE IN:

INT. HUT - DAY

A grizzled HAG in black cape and pointed hat stirs a huge cauldron with an oar. She sniffs suspiciously, and turns to a glowing computer screen on a bench.

> HAG
> Eye of newt . . . high adenine DNA . . . third derivative power function . . . .

She glances back at the cauldron, yanks the oar around, and returns to the computer. She jabs a key, then grabs a jar.

> HAG
> What gender, I'd like to know. A dead virgin's ear, but they never—

Her finger stops at a spot on the screen.

> HAG
> Oh, it don't matter. Fancy that.

She pulls a wrinkled, ear-shaped thing from the jar, drops it on the open computer CD tray, and shoves in the tray. Then she bashes it closed with the butt of the oar.

A bolt of crimson stabs from the screen to the cauldron. The fluid erupts in a fountain of brownish-green slime.

And then the slime is gone, the fire beneath the cauldron is out, and a handsome MAN in a tuxedo stands in the swaying cauldron, barely keeping his balance.

He throws out his arms to the Hag, a radiant smile blossoming on his face.

                    MAN
          Baby!

The Hag looks from the computer to the Man a couple of times, then grins and tosses her oar aside.

                    NARRATOR (V.O.)
          Macrohard—the leading source of sorcerous
          sorceress software.

FADE TO BLACK

THE PIRATE BALLERINA

The bells in the towers of Mark-on-Sea stirred
And woke all the people around.
Two kittens quit stalking a cow when they heard,
And slunk off to check on the sound.

"To arms," cried a sentry. "Marauders in sight.
A flag with a lavender skull."
The ship growing large in the new morning light
Had toeshoes adorning its hull.

"Alas," cried the Mayor, "Alas and Alack."
"Oh, shut up," his goodwife replied.
"We've quite enough trouble with Pirate McCack;
Just leave your two kittens outside."

The sentries sought weapons and whiskey and pluck;
The farmers relaxed with a sigh.
But craftsmen all knew they had run out of luck:
The dread ballerina was nigh.

While parents told children to hide in their beds
The children ignored their behest,
For dreams of Melissa McCack filled their heads
And pride she would soon be their guest.

The ship rode the breeze to the sea-wall and turned.
Beyond stood the gate to the town.
A sucking, a slapping—the water, it churned.
A creak and the gangplank came down.

A silence descended, the town held in check;
The crew of the ship went below.
A gasp broke the stillness. McCack came on deck.
She smiled and started to glow.

She leapt to the roof of the cabin back aft
And danced till the guardsmen went blind.
She spun in a pink satin tutu. Her craft
Belied what her crew had in mind.

She swung off the end of the mizzenmast spar,
On town wall alighted and twirled.
Her dancing, so frantic, raised wind from afar,
And all of their flags came unfurled.

The children stood quiet, their parents like rock.
The pirate abducted all eyes.
She danced to the portal and turned the great lock;
Her crew skipped inside for their prize.

"Oh, stop them!" the Mayor cried, hands on his face.
He tripped on his cat, though, and saw
McCack whirling past with a style and grace
That froze him in impotent awe.

The crew of the pirate ship looted and stole.
They took what they needed and more.
But wives of the craftsmen considered the whole
Procedure an insolent bore.

Twelve pumpkins they pilfered; three lambs and a
sow;
Six barrels of wine and a ham.
A brace of the chickens; a sickly old cow;
Some flour; four beakers of jam.

'Twas terrible really, the havoc they wreaked,
That miscreant toe-dancing crew.
The tide of their filching rose quickly and peaked,
Then ebbed till they finally were through.

They left behind "payment," star sapphires and such;
Cheap rocks from their hideout back west.
Such baubles the farmers thought quite a nice touch,
But craftsmen stood raging, depressed:

No bracelets, no silverware taken as spoils,
No ironwork, dresses, or gold.
No trinkets were scattered to cover *their* toils,
While farmers grew brazen and bold.

A sob broke the hush as the ship pulled away,
Its prow beating waves into foam.
Two cats on the gunwale grinned back o'er the bay;
The Mayor just sighed and went home.

The craftsmen hope Mark-on-Sea peaceful will stay,
Yet worry McCack will return.
There's nothing disgusting as pirates who pay—
Especially more than they earn.

RUNAWAY

FADE IN:

INT. LIVING ROOM - DAY

PAPA enters and plops in an easy chair opposite MOMMA, dropping his briefcase. Momma knits.

> MOMMA
> Good evening, dear.

> PAPA
> Evening. How's the day?

> MOMMA
> Oh, same as always. Except the Pierces next door had a fire.

> PAPA
> I wondered about the pile of ash.

> MOMMA
> The plumbing needs a little work.

> PAPA
> That could explain the swamp out front.

> MOMMA
> Oh, yes, and our son ran away.

> PAPA
> Who, Richard?

MOMMA

Well, that being our only child and all, I think it was him, yes.

PAPA

Strange. He always seemed so stable.

MOMMA

He did have a few tendencies.

PAPA

Not the action figures again.

MOMMA

They were dolls, dear.

PAPA

They were soldiers. Tough guys. Very macho.

MOMMA

He put them in dresses.

PAPA

That only showed his interest in girls. Healthy, that.

MOMMA

He never mastered peeing while standing up.

PAPA

Hmmm, that did seem odd.

MOMMA

And this year it got bad at school.

PAPA

Why's that?

MOMMA
Seventh grade, I'm afraid. Gym class.

PAPA
Yes?

MOMMA
Common showers.

PAPA
What of it? Surely you don't think that brought out unhealthy tendencies?

MOMMA
The other boys started teasing him about missing his twiggie.

PAPA
Oh. Oh, yes. I could see where that might be a problem.

MOMMA
Then he borrowed your anatomy book.

PAPA
What? I kept that locked up.

MAMA
And he snuck off to the zoo.

PAPA
No.

MOMMA
Yes. I'm afraid he knows he's not the son we always wanted.

PAPA
But—

MOMMA
He's figured out he's a girl.

PAPA
My god.

MOMMA
It gets worse.

PAPA
How could it get worse?

MOMMA
When he cracked your safe, he found the note pinned to his diaper.

PAPA
You mean, when he was in the dumpster?

MOMMA
That's the one.

PAPA
Surely you threw that out . . .

MOMMA
It had sentimental value.

PAPA
His mother said he was the most obnoxious, bawling brat she ever saw.

MOMMA
Well, there was that.

PAPA

After fifteen other kids, all girls, she was naming it Richard whether it liked it or not.

MOMMA

I remember.

PAPA

And she hoped it had the decency to shut up and die before anyone found it.

MOMMA

Good thing you were looking for your mother that night.

PAPA

What part of that note could you possible find sentimental?

MOMMA

Well, she gave the child a name.

PAPA

Ah. Right. So we had to raise it as a son. Once started—

MOMMA

He was only two days old.

PAPA

—got to carry it through.

MOMMA

Or "she."

PAPA

Too late for that.

MOMMA
Nurture over nature, huh? Environment outweighs genetics?

PAPA
Certainly.

MOMMA
So we hoped. But what if he decides to become a girl now?

PAPA
That could be a problem.

MOMMA
Yes. Expensive things, girls.

PAPA
Hmmm.

MOMMA
Well, there's pot roast when you're hungry.

PAPA
Ah, good. Now who could that be?

RICHARD enters, dressed in a smart suit with ascot and bob haircut.

RICHARD
Hello, Momma, Papa. I've figured it out.

PAPA
Glad you're back, boy.

MOMMA
What's that, sweetie?

RICHARD
I'm joining a club for men who've had sex change operations and then become lesbians.

MOMMA
Lesbians?

RICHARD
And I'll be the butch one.

PAPA
Well, as long as you're still dating girls.

MOMMA
And we don't have to buy new clothes.

RICHARD
Just don't call me "Dickie" anymore.

Momma and Papa nod in sage agreement.

FADE TO BLACK

MACROHARD #6

FADE IN:

EXT. HIGHWAY - DAY

A convertible is adrift in a sea of automobiles, inching along, its top down. Exit signs abound, and another sign proclaims "Speed Limit 55."

INT. CAR

A MAN in the passenger seat rips up a map and throws it out. The WOMAN driver glares at him.

>   WOMAN
> Stick to the beltway, you said.

>   MAN
> So take the back roads. I don't care.

>   WOMAN
> One-twenty-three is not a back road.

A BEARDED MAN in the back CHUCKLES.

>   BEARDED MAN
> Don't matter. Whatever happens, it's always the driver's fault.

The Woman glances back at him. The Man beside her laughs, and she grins ruefully.

>   MAN
> Car pool rules.

A withered CRONE in the back reaches forward, handing the Man a COMPACT DISK. He raises an eyebrow and slides it into the player. A CD VOICE blares out.

> CD (V.O.)
> Take one twenty-three *now*. They just closed the beltway for an overturned fuel truck.

The Woman gapes at the CD player, then peels out of traffic onto the exit ramp. She looks at the man beside her.

> CD (V.O.)
> Veer right, take the alley. Watch for the pedestrian.

The Woman peals into an alley. The second she turns, a crash snarls up route one-twenty-three.

A HOMELESS MAN trips over some trash. The woman slams on the brakes, then maneuvers around him.

> WOMAN
> What on earth . . . ?

> CD (V.O.)
> In other news, that fast-moving storm is about to let go over Washington.

> MAN
> Quick, top up.

The sky darkens, and rain pelts down on the car, as the roof slowly rises into position. The Woman twists to look back at the crone.

        WOMAN
Where did you get that CD?

The Crone grins.

        NARRATOR (V.O.)
Macrohard—the leading edge in real-time news technology.

FADE TO BLACK

DOING DUTY

FADE IN:

INT. AIRPORT - DAY

BILL fidgets in a customs line at a small airport. People surround him: another line to his left, and a few on his right. A sign reads "International Arrivals."

At the counter ahead stand two customs AGENTS, GILBERT and CARLA, under another sign reading, "DECLARE GOODS—It's Your DUTY."

The FROWSY WOMAN in front of Bill plunks two bottles of wine on the counter.

>   FROWSY WOMAN
> What's the duty on these?

>   AGENT GILBERT
> Two dollars apiece.

>   FROWSY WOMAN
> These are vintage. It's gotta be more than that.

>   AGENT CARLA
> Sorry, ma'am. Cheap wine.

>   AGENT GILBERT
> You got had.

The Frowsy Woman huffs, throws four dollar bills on the counter, and stalks forward past the agents.

At the wall to the left, near the agents, a CARPENTER dumps a load of tools—drill, extension cord, tool chest, and cooler. She opens the cooler and stuffs a sandwich in her mouth.

Bill reaches the customs counter. He pulls out a flintlock pistol and points it at the agents.

> BILL
> Gimme—

> AGENT GILBERT
> Would you look at that.

> AGENT CARLA
> Haven't seen one of them in years.

> BILL
> Give me your—

> AGENT GILBERT
> Pre-war, I believe.

> BILL
> —money—

> AGENT CARLA
> Pre-*Revolutionary* War.

> AGENT GILBERT
> That's what I meant.

> BILL
> What are you . . . ? Give me—

> AGENT CARLA
> Patience, dear. That's a valuable piece.

                    AGENT GILBERT
Don't want to undercharge you, now do we?

                    BILL
You can't . . . what? I said—

                    AGENT CARLA
Passport, please.

The man gapes. Agent Gilbert plucks a passport out
of his pocket and opens it.

                    AGENT GILBERT
Ah. Hello, Bill.

The Carpenter's drill WHINES into action. Bill
winces. A TEENAGE GIRL behind Bill peaks
around at the fuss. The BOY with her dances to silent
music, headphones on his ears.

                    TEENAGE GIRL
               (interested)
He's got a gun.

The Boy dances on.

                    BILL
You don't underst—

                    AGENT CARLA
Now, now, don't panic.

                    AGENT GILBERT
We get fake passports all the time.

                    BILL
It's not . . .

Bill stares, impotent. The Teenage Girl hauls the Boy around and points at the gun. She yells into his ear, past the headphones.

                TEENAGE GIRL
        Gun.

The Boy bops his head in the general direction of Bill, then looks at the girl.

                BOY
        Retro, baby.

The drill stops and the Carpenter HAMMERS twice, sharply; BANGS echo off the walls. Bill cringes, spinning around. The Teenage Girl plucks the gun from his hand.

                TEENAGE GIRL
        Turkish.

                BOY
        Horseman's pistol, I do believe.

Bill looks around wildly, then snatches vainly at the gun. He appears uncertain whether to cringe and run, or go for the gun, so he alternates.

                AGENT CARLA
        Come now, we can't assess it till we see it.

The Boy takes the gun and hefts it, then turns away and waves it at the BUSINESS MAN behind him.

                BOY
        Good balance.

The Business Man takes it and scrutinizes it. Bill flails past the Boy toward the Man.

>BUSINESS MAN
>Scratched up. Oughta take better care of it.

A PRIM WOMAN behind him snatches the gun just before Bill gets to it. She tips out the cylinder and dumps a bullet on the floor, then dry fires it.

>PRIM WOMAN
>Nice action. No spark. Needs new flint.

Bill dives to the floor and scoops up the bullet, a horrified expression on his face. The Prim Woman tosses the gun across the room to a FAT LADY.

>PRIM WOMAN
>Hey, Mabel, this is smooth enough for you.

The Fat Lady snags the gun mid-air with one finger through the trigger guard. She spins it around and aims it at Bill as he runs toward her, stuffing the bullet in his pocket. He stops cold. She dry fires it. He flinches.

>FAT LADY
>You're right.

Bill dives toward the gun. Just before he gets there, a KID on a skate board whizzes past, grabs the gun by its barrel, and dodges between passengers.

The Kid holds the gun like a hand-ax and waves it around. Bill pursues, angling to cut him off.

A YOUNG GIRL sticks out her foot and trips the Kid. He goes sprawling. The gun flies over Bill's leaping, outstretched fingers. The Carpenter SAWS in the background.

> YOUNG GIRL
> (to kid)
> Mom told you to stop that.

The gun sails overhead and lands in a trash can near the duty station with the two Agents. A JANITOR reaches to pull out the plastic liner and sees the gun.

He plucks it out, shrugs, and stuffs it his pocket as Bill stumbles up.

> BILL
> Give it ba—

> JANITOR
> Finders keepers.

The Janitor yanks out the plastic bag of trash and turns toward Bill, forcing him back. The Young Girl whizzes by on the Kid's skateboard; the Kid chases behind.

> KID
> Give it back.

The Young Girl looks over her shoulder.

> YOUNG GIRL
> Mom didn't say *I* couldn't ride it.

The Young Girl takes a U-turn around a stanchion, watching the Kid.

The Janitor twirls the trash bag at Bill. Not looking, the Young Girl smashes into the bag.

Trash flies everywhere.

> JANITOR
> Not again.

He bends to recover the garbage. Bill hops beside him and snags the gun from his pocket. Bill waves it overhead, backing toward the customs counter.

> BILL
> All right, everybody, this is a—

Agent Gilbert reaches over the table and snatches the gun from Bill's hand.

> AGENT GILBERT
> —late model, maybe 1810. We know.

Bill spins, horrified anew. Agent Carla takes the gun, caressing it.

> AGENT CARLA
> Lots of duty on this baby.

> AGENT GILBERT
> Hope you're rich.

Bill backs away, but is pushed forward by the Teenage Girl, the Boy, the Business Man, and the Janitor. Bill struggles but can't get away.

> AGENT CARLA
> Unless you want to sell it.

The CROWD goes still. The Carpenter DRILLS some more. Agent Gilbert looks at Agent Carla.

> AGENT GILBERT
> Worth a ton.

> BUSINESS MAN
> I bid one.

Bill's jaw drops.

> AGENT CARLA
> One point five.

> TEENAGE GIRL
> Two.

> BOY
> I think they're in thousands.

> TEENAGE GIRL
> Oh. Sorry.

Bill looks around frantically, still blocked in.

> JANITOR
> Two, then.

> AGENT CARLA
> Two point five.

> BUSINESS MAN
> Too rich for me, dammit.

He turns away. The Crowd behind Bill thins slightly.

> AGENT GILBERT
Going once.

> FAT LADY
> (to Bill)
You did want to sell it, right?

Bill gasps, eyes whipping from left to right.

> AGENT GILBERT
Going twice.

The Young Girl busts up the Crowd around Bill, darting through carrying the skateboard. The Kid scrambles after.

> KID
Give it back! Give it back!

> AGENT GILBERT
Sold.

The Carpenter drops a load of timber with a loud BANG. Bill jumps. Agent Carla opens the cash register and pulls out currency. Bill stares at her hands.

> AGENT GILBERT
What are you doing?

> AGENT CARLA
Think I carry that kind of cash?

> AGENT GILBERT
But that's—

> AGENT CARLA
> You know I'm good for it.

Agent Gilbert rolls his eyes. Agent Carla dumps a pile of money before Bill. He hesitates, then grabs it all in great wads without counting it and stuffs it in his pockets.

> AGENT CARLA
> You had a bullet?

> BILL
> Oh, uh . . .

Bill digs in one pocket while still stuffing money in another. He tosses the bullet on the table. Agent Carla lovingly loads her new gun.

Bill grabs the last of the money and fights through the Crowd.

> TEENAGE GIRL
> Good deal, man.

The Business Man shakes his head.

> BUSINESS MAN
> Worth more, even rusty.

Bill shoves past them. The Carpenter HAMMERS twice. Bill freezes, arms up.

> CARPENTER
> Oops.

The wall near the Agents tilts inward.

AGENT GILBERT
Not again.

Agent Carla grabs the pistol and yanks Agent Gilbert to the side. Other AGENTS and TRAVELERS dive away. The wall collapses in a cloud of dust, wiping out two customs counters.

Bill yanks his arms back down and looks around guiltily.

Agent Gilbert pushes up through a pile of debris. He reaches down and pulls up Agent Carla. People scramble up all over.

The Carpenter clutches tools to her chest, peers over her shoulder, and skulks away.

Agent Carla points to the shattered cash register, laying amidst the fallen wall.

AGENT CARLA
On the bright side, maybe we could say the money was stolen.

Agent Gilbert looks at the cash register.

AGENT GILBERT
Some idiot robbing customs agents. Think anybody'd buy it?

They look at each other.

AGENTS GILBERT AND CARLA
(in unison)
Naaaahhhhhhhh.

Agent Carla lifts up the gun and they both admire it. Agent Gilbert tries to grab it, and they BICKER.

Beyond them, Bill dashes off.

FADE TO BLACK

MACROHARD #9

FADE IN:

INT. LIVING ROOM - DAY

NANCY enters, hands fluttering, eyes darting from bookcase to couch to DVD player. She stops.

> NANCY
> Darn it, Maria Carlotta Francesca, you show yourself this minute.

She lunges past the TV set and looks down, then shoots over to the couch and leans over.

> NANCY
> I'm sick and tired of this. Every Saturday night.

She opens a closet and peers in, then disappears down a hall.

> NANCY (O.S.)
> Maria Carlotta Francesca, you either come get your bath or I'm gonna make the SPCA's "Most Wanted" list.

Nancy storms back into the room, looks around again, snorts. She walks over to a computer and sits.

She taps a few keys and the screen glows. Her fingers slide a mouse around. She enters the words "Maria Carlotta Francesca."

On the screen, the Earth hangs in a mist of stars. It spins slowly, then stops over North America.

The continent expands rapidly, centering on the Chesapeake area, then Washington D.C., then suburban streets with houses and trees.

The image keeps expanding until the bushes in a ten-by-fifteen foot area beside a house occupy the whole screen.

The bushes on the screen slide along. A rustling is obvious in one bush. The image expands, down through the branches, and then—a CAT is revealed.

>   NANCY
> Gotcha!

She gets up and charges out the front door. From outside comes a MEOW.

>   NANCY (O.S.)
> No, you do not get a prize. You get a bath, you obtuse fur-ball. How dare you sneak around like a . . . no, I do not want your mouse. I like the kind with wires.

Nancy comes back in, cradling the Cat.

>   NARRATOR (V.O.)
> Macrohard—the leading edge in real-time cartography.

FADE TO BLACK

ONCE A BITCH

I LEAPT THROUGH the opening and landed on all fours in the two-legger den. A strange place it was, larger than most caves, with flat walls and sharp corners. A dead, moss-like material blanketed the ground—no, they called it floor—and stiff, unnatural wooden things were scattered at random. Nothing moved except the pattering of mice behind the walls, a reassuring sound. Distant voices—laughter, a scuffle—nothing I could make out. I prided myself on knowing two-leggers, but their speech was often beyond me, especially so far away.

Safe enough. But too much light, perhaps, with a full moon. I went back to the opening. The window. I was in two-legger territory, I should use their words. Why else had I studied them all those years? I scratched at one wooden covering with a paw and pulled it across the window. It took too long and made a raucous squeal, so I snarled at the other and left it.

I crouched in the far corner of the room, behind a low, flat-topped table-thing, though it wasn't really a table; walls surrounded three sides and most of a fourth, with a cave-like opening in the middle of the fourth side and a chair jammed into the opening. I scraped the thong of my spell-pouch over my head and let the leather bag fall to the floor. Good hoofer hide, that pouch. It was a shame to rip the seams; they took so long to stitch, with tooth and needle and uncured skin. But it was the only way my kind could carry liquids. Only the two-leggers have hands.

I stopped. A howl. But not the self-respecting, deep-throated roar of my kind. A soprano yelp, more like. A *domestic*.

There is nothing worse than domestics. Dogs. The traitors of the canine world. Even cats aren't as bad, though I never let them get close. And this feeble excuse for a mutt was particularly obnoxious. He was the reason I was here. It was bad enough going into heat when I was hungry and trying to hunt. It was bad enough putting up with the aggravation of my own kind, when my body betrayed my wishes with its needs. But to be caught in the woods outside this two-legger town by a mangy mongrel, a brainless under-sized domestic!

At least it hadn't taken. I wasn't ready for another load of pups.

Another yelp, closer. I hurried. I was still in heat, and the dog might smell me. I needed to change, find some two-legger body coverings, and get out, so I could make a proper entrance at the edge of this settlement without arousing their suspicion. And then I could study these upright, arrogant creatures from their own point of view, and figure out some fitting revenge for the mutt.

I ripped the pouch with my teeth, spilling the potion. The stupid floor was lapping it up before I could. I jabbed my tongue into the bag and slurped up what I could. Claws, I'd worked for days on that stinking slop; seasons, if I counted all the earlier research. Maybe I was more adept at magic than my pack-mates, but apparently I was also more clumsy. I tore another corner of the bag in my haste.

Voices, coming closer. The dog led them to me, worthless creature that he was, so he must have caught my scent. I really hadn't thought he was that good. I'd get even, though . . . if there was enough potion left.

The pouch had been ready for over a moon, actually. I'd long intended to try this spell. These two-leggers were the only other intelligent species I knew of, and I longed to learn more of them. The chance to couple my visit with revenge on the dog was the irresistible bait that brought me here tonight.

I sucked on the soft flooring, ripped the leather, chewed and sucked. There had to be enough.

More noises. Two-leggers gathered outside, beyond the window, and more by the door to this room. I was trapped. They muttered amongst themselves. Something about spirit-walkers, which was laughable, and wolves, which of course was all too true. Perhaps they'd seen my tracks, though that hardly seemed likely on the rock-hard ground. I glanced out the window. The moon reflected off the long, sharp teeth they carried in their hands. Mother of Midnight, what kind of animal could such fangs have been ripped from? And where did they live? Every two-legger was armed, but I'd never heard of a beast with such teeth.

The door rattled. Desperation. I ripped up the floor, some fur-like piece of it, and found wood beneath, another layer of floor. I swallowed the soaked, disgusting mass, bit the chair and yanked it out of the way, and cowered in the opening beneath the table-thing.

The door burst open. Several shouting two-leggers stormed into the room carrying fire-sticks, lighting up the place like twilight. One of them held the straining, whining dog by its collar. I'd run out of time. But I'd take a few down with me, hopefully that mutt among them. For I was Silverdust, and I always did my share and more, for the pride of the pack.

Suddenly, my guts tore me inside out. The room blurred, the shouts of the searchers blinked and took on a strange new timber, and all the scents faded. My whole body writhed and itched and wrinkled, twitched and twisted with an agony I could scarcely credit. I whimpered, I think; from somewhere came an anguished cry. Muffled footsteps approached, but nothing sounded right. With a final jerk, the pain stopped, and I opened my eyes again.

To see the hated snout of the traitor domestic but a tail's length away. And then the long, slender weapons of the two-leggers, as they came up behind their pet.

I sprang. No time to set or aim, just attack, and sort out the bodies later.

Something went wrong—my legs, balance . . . everything. My head smashed into the bottom of the table above, the whole thing crashed over backwards, the two-leggers shouted, I thrust out a foreleg for balance . . . and my body betrayed me again as I fell helpless at the feet of my foes. The last thing I saw, as my mind faded black, was the approaching, slobbering snout of the enemy domestic—and what it did when it reached me.

The benighted dog licked my face.

I CAME TO not long after; the moon still rode the stars. I lay in a bed, and two-leggers swarmed the room, looking more confused than angry. They hadn't killed me, or even bound me with their hated ropes. More fool they.

I turned on my side and pulled up my hind legs to kick off the heavy cloth things they'd covered me with—and came face to face with the domestic. Again.

I paused. The two-leggers had put up their weapons, but the mongrel still had its teeth, and it had the advantage of position. I hesitated, calculating.

It yipped and grinned.

Unbelievable. I lost any concern about the ignorant beast. I pulled up a forepaw to swipe the insolent upstart's nose—and froze, staring, memory returning. The sight shook me to the bowels.

My forepaw . . . wasn't mine. It was naked, like the claw of a bird.

No, not a bird. That wasn't what the potion did.

A hand.

By all the winds and storms, a hand. I'd done it. I'd become a two-legger. And I obviously had all their slowness of thought, for I was stunned, gazing at the hand, until the dog wormed his way forward and stuck his head under it, begging to be petted, licking my face again.

I jerked back at a sound from the two-leggers.

Laughter. And babbling, something about 'poor girl' and 'starving.'

Astonishing. They'd gone from armed hostiles, to neutral, to accepting me, all on the strength of this dog's reaction. I hardly knew what to do. I'd meant to fit in, to infiltrate the town and gain my revenge on this domestic . . . yet here I'd been caught breaking in. Clearly, they hadn't seen me until I'd changed, or they'd know me for a spell-user. But still, I'd have expected fear, or attack, or anything but laughter. And now I owed a debt to this stupid mutt, perhaps for keeping me alive.

Claws and Teeth, what a night.

THE MEASURE OF my deformation—or transformation, for it *was* intentional—only slowly dawned on me over the next few days. The walking was weird, the clothes obnoxious. My beautiful fur coat was gone, replaced by the body of a plucked fowl, for all its aesthetic appeal. The language was surprising, so many words I hadn't known, and shades of meaning my kind never used. I'm certain the two-leggers thought me a mind-puppy, for all my ignorance. Where I came from I never said, and even that they accepted, as if I'd had an accident to cause forgetfulness. Such gullible creatures they were. And far too trusting of their fool domestic. He kept following me around, and I daren't do anything so long as he helped deflect any doubts they might have about me.

The biggest shock was my hands. The things these, um, humans did were far beyond my wildest dreams. Eating, and fighting, and making things. And writing—what a strange and delightful idea. Far beyond my crude picture-knowledge. They didn't know the kinds of magic I knew, and most of them seemed to fear it when I asked, but they had memories and skills of their own which I absorbed like the dust swallows rain.

The first task I set myself, of course, was to dig a path of retreat, though it took a while. I learned from my readings where they kept their herbs and such, the reagents of my spells, and I quietly collected what I needed. I despaired once, unable to find a key mushroom, but the writings of one obscure book, lost in the basement of an abandoned dwelling, lent me a suitable alternative. Not a simple 'like-to-like' transformation, but a 'return to condition of before.' It would do. I added a snip of head-hair and a clipping of toenail to the basic reagents, to define the essence of myself, tossed in the secondary roots suggested by the book, and let it bake in the sun in a clay pot for half a moon. My escape potion completed, I hid it in an old leather flagon in the room they assigned me. (I threw out the wine first, a warped flavor I tried but once, to the amusement of my hostess. It tasted too much like my potion.)

Then one night, almost two moons after my change, I learned a different use for hands.

I'd often been told I was a lovely female by these humans, but that had seemed merely a pointless observation, once I got used to being without fur. I'd been a healthy wolf, after all. Why not an equally well-built human? Something else was at work, however, which they hadn't mentioned. One night, I learned about caressing.

As it happened, no humans had ever coupled in my presence, and I hadn't thought much of it. They took longer to raise their young, after all, so at first I assumed the females, the women, went into heat but seldom. Besides which, the women hinted at some odd taboo about coupling in front of others. I supposed it was because they did it so rarely.

Not quite right. Not even close. It turns out these human bodies are almost *always* ready for pupping, with cycles once a moon. So then I couldn't understand their taboo at all. But in any event, my stay was delightfully free of such distractions, and I expected the situation to continue.

Claws, was I wrong. One night, a man the females had often warned me of came to my room. I was curious, for they had said he was very important, a bad one to cross, and I should avoid him. They maybe; not I. Besides, it was a strange time of the day for visitors, so I welcomed him in. He'd always been friendly before, and taught me of their weapons, which turned out not to be teeth at all, but something made from rocks and fire. Or so he said. But I had no second thoughts as he entered and shut the door behind him.

Then it was like he'd taken a potion himself, the way he changed. A 'wolf,' the women had called him, much to my amusement, but now I learned where they thought the term came from. A pity they didn't take the lesson a step further. For what must a wolf expect if he seeks one-sided sex?

A bitch.

It took me a few seconds to realize what he was after, though. This human mind—so thorough, so *slow*. But he didn't come up behind me the way I would have expected; he simply pushed me down on the bed and kept facing me, explaining new words. Like 'caress.'

Well, I knew when I was interested, and when I wasn't, and I asked him to leave. He smiled and continued, and I became most annoyed to find my body thought it was interested. I started responding, part of me screaming I was a fool, when a low growl came from under a chair.

That stupid domestic had snuck into my room.

The man paused, then left me. He grabbed the chair and chased the dog out the door, kicking it all the way. I stood, hating to feel sorry for the mutt, glad of the reprieve, confused at how I could possibly side with that four-legged traitor. The man slammed the door, turned, and stalked up to me again. He clearly intended to pick up where he'd left off. But he had allowed me to cool, and now I had my body back under control.

I bared my teeth and snarled, fingers crooked into claws. He laughed. I launched myself at his throat, batting his arms aside, scratching and biting and yelling at him to get out, leave me alone, I didn't want him there. He bashed me with his curled hand, hard. It hurt. I wasn't used to fighting that way, and my teeth were all but useless. Worse, after only two moons, I still hadn't mastered this body nearly as well as he knew his own.

He laughed again. He thought it was a game, as well he might. Amongst wolves, if a bitch doesn't want to be mounted, she won't be.

He pushed me down on the bed again, but now my body no longer felt like betraying me. I sagged, as if giving in, and slithered to the floor when he relaxed his grip. I dove for the window; he yanked back my ankle and I collapsed beside the table. I rolled into the little cave under the table, thinking 'desk,' furious my stupid human brain could be cataloguing words at a time like this. He clutched my clothes and dragged me back out.

Then I kicked him. Where he hadn't kicked the dog. It wasn't really intentional, merely the only open target. He howled, cringing, holding himself with one hand, grabbing for a knife at his belt and swearing vendettas on my family for generations to come.

Well, that was too much. If he wanted coupling and was willing to fight for it, that was one thing. But threatening the pack was another.

I rolled to the side as his knife ripped the carpet. I kicked it from his hand, sprang for the cabinet across the room, and grabbed the leather flagon. My return trip. It would take but a second. I turned to face him, grinning in anticipation.

And his curled hand exploded in my face. I hadn't even heard him approach.

He grabbed the flagon as I fell, jerking it from my grasp with a sneer, daring to thank me for my hospitable offer. I clawed the bed, trying to rise. He bit out the stopper and tilted the bottle into his mouth.

I couldn't stop him. My first thought was panic—I wouldn't be fighting a man, now, but a wolf. Yet that was wrong; he'd be helpless after the change. I despaired of my own return, until I remembered how easy it was to mix reagents as a human. I could make another potion any time. I shook my head, but my mind stayed foggy and slow.

Then the transformation took him.

He shrieked in anguish. It was awful. I'm not sure I'd ever have changed, myself, if I'd known it looked that bad. But I had no sympathy for his plight. If this human wanted to play wolf, I could think of no more fitting reward for his desires.

When it was finished, the new beast whimpered and tried to crawl away, as uncoordinated as I had first been. I rolled across the bed and went to the window. I grabbed a chair and smashed it into the frame, leaving me a solid stick when chair and shutters shattered. I will never forget the expression on the wolf's face as I stumbled forward, smiled, and bashed its head.

I could have hit it harder. Lupine skulls are thicker than the human variety. But it was enough. I hauled the limp form to the window and pulled off its remaining clothes. It was awake enough to paw at me, but too befuddled to bite. Just as I went to heave it outside, the door of my room burst in.

I guess I should have expected it. The whole house-family was there. They saw the man's clothes, they saw the wolf, and they saw me. "Witch!" they cried. "Enchantress!" They wove patterns in the air with their hands, and a couple of them snatched out short blades.

I hissed and lunged, waving my stick, and the idiots tumbled over themselves to back away. Amazing how fickle the human mind. I crushed a couple of wrists, slammed the door, and threw the bolt. I raced to the window, snatched up the man's knife, heaved out my canine, and followed it to the ground. Then I grasped the edge of the window again, pulled myself up, reached in, and grabbed the man's cloak. A poor substitute for fur, but I had little choice.

I wrestled my creation onto my shoulders, held its legs, and trotted to the edge of the burg. The townsmen wouldn't follow, not at night. That much I knew of humans before ever I joined them. Once in the trees, I dumped my burden by a stream and splashed its face. When it roused enough to stagger to its feet and wobble, I left it. It would survive. I didn't want it to die. That would have spoiled the revenge.

At last I was free to go. But I hadn't taken two paces down the trail before I halted, staring at the animal which stepped from the shadows, blocking my retreat.

That same, ubiquitous *domestic.*

It panted and grinned, pleased as a pup. I turned to take a different path; it followed. What could I do? I owed it too much to wish it ill any longer.

Then I knew.

I led it back to the floundering wolf. The dog barked once, but I kept using the word of the humans, that magic word 'friend.' The domestic settled down and began sniffing at the sorry beast. When I finally snuck away, hiding my scent in the stream, the two looked to be together for quite a while. And not at the wolf's choosing.

I chuckled. My creation was in for such a rude surprise. I vaulted onto a rock and scrambled up a small hill, pausing to enjoy the squabbling behind me. It wouldn't be long now.

For you see, my new spell didn't change the creature and keep everything else the same. That would have taken the mushroom I couldn't find. This was, instead, that stronger spell I'd found, easier and quicker with the plants available this time of year. So my potion didn't turn the man into the kind of wolf he might actually like to be. It could only make him into the kind which I had been.

The noises behind me peaked, the howls of the domestic crowning the feeble complaints of the wolf. I gave it up, and laughed out loud. It really was too perfect.

For my creation was a bitch.

RETURNING GOODS

FADE IN:

INT. STORE - DAY

MR. RATHBURTON, a well-dressed gentleman, walks up to the counter of a small knickknack shop. Baroque little clocks, coasters, vases, and less useful items litter the shelves.

Behind the counter, a bespectacled, mousy MR. CUTHBERT neatly stacks up tiny silver boxes.

                    RATHBURTON
          Good morning. I'd like to—

                    CUTHBERT
          Hello. I'm Mr. Cuthbert.

                    RATHBURTON
               (beat)
          Yes. It says that out front. I'd like to—

                    CUTHBERT
          What's your name?

                    RATHBURTON
               (beat)
          I'm Rathburton. From the Navy Department. I'd like to—

                    CUTHBERT
          Ooh, that's nifty. Rathburton and Cuthbert. Got a ring, don't you think?

Rathburton stares at him a moment.

> RATHBURTON
> May I speak?

> CUTHBERT
> Certainly. I love to hear my customers.

> RATHBURTON
> Good. I'd like to—

> CUTHBERT
> It's how I do business, you see. Don't know what people want if they don't tell me—

> RATHBURTON
> Would you shut up?

Cuthbert splatters silver boxes all over. He looks forlornly from them to Rathburton, opens his mouth, then shuts it.

> RATHBURTON
> Thank you. I have something to return.

> CUTHBERT
> Oh, that's sad. Didn't work? Wrong color? They already had one?

> RATHBURTON
> No, it works fine. We just don't need it.

> CUTHBERT
> Need?

He looks around at his merchandise.

> CUTHBERT
> What's need got to do with it?

> RATHBURTON
> This is a model.

He pulls a model of a submarine from under his coat and sets it on the counter. Cuthbert frowns.

> CUTHBERT
> It certainly is. You want to return it, then?

> RATHBURTON
> Not the model, no. The real thing.

Cuthbert looks from Rathburton to the model.

> CUTHBERT
> A submarine?

> RATHBURTON
> Yes.

Cuthbert looks around at his merchandise. He gives Rathburton a strange look.

> CUTHBERT
> I don't think we carry those.

> RATHBURTON
> I'm aware of that. But you do take all returns.

Cuthbert just looks at him. Rathburton pulls a full-page newspaper sheet from his jacket and unfolds it.

RATHBURTON
It says right in your ad. You'll take back anything, even if not purchased here.

Cuthbert leans over and glances at the ad.

CUTHBERT
Yes. It says that. But I expected a bit of common—

RATHBURTON
I *am* from the Government. There are truth in advertising laws.

Cuthbert gets slightly agitated.

CUTHBERT
But you can't expect me to—

RATHBURTON
Where would you like it?

CUTHBERT
You mean it's . . .

Cuthbert panics. He runs to the window and looks out. Then he looks back at Rathburton, confused. Rathburton points upward.

Cuthbert looks upward out the window. He SCREECHES and flinches back, clutching the window frame. His eyes travel slowly from far left to far right. He glares at Rathburton.

CUTHBERT
How can you lift it?

RATHBURTON
Special cranes. Lots of them. It's only four hundred feet long.

Cuthbert looks up again.

CUTHBERT
Four . . . hundred . . .

RATHBURTON
We'll take cash, or a refund on our National Debt card.

He waves a credit card. Cuthbert keeps looking up. Then he frowns.

CUTHBERT
It's old. I see rust.

RATHBURTON
Yes, it has a few hundred thousand miles on it. But we keep our subs good as new.

Cuthbert's jaw firms. He marches back to the counter, grabs the newspaper, and jabs his finger at some fine print.

CUTHBERT
Depreciation. Right there. You don't get full price for used goods.

Rathburton purses his lips, then nods.

RATHBURTON
That's fair. Whatever the taxpayer can get is fine.

Cuthbert gets a gleam in his eye. He glances toward the window again, then pulls out a form and starts jotting things down.

CUTHBERT
Let's see, new price was what? A couple—

RATHBURTON
Seven hundred million.

Cuthbert looks taken aback.

CUTHBERT
Dollars?

RATHBURTON
It ain't rubles.

CUTHBERT
Right. Seven, zero, zero, zero, zero . . . .

He taps his finger, counting silently.

CUTHBERT
OK. There's wear and tear, fair use tax, reverse state tax, restocking fee . . .

He glances at Rathburton, who waits patiently. Cuthbert gets a sly gleam in his eye and mumbles more and more quietly, peeking up at Rathburton now and then.

CUTHBERT
. . . then there's transport charges, handling fee, import/export duty, excise . . .

He mumbles some more, scratching notes. He draws a line, fiddles with a calculator, and writes down another figure. He bites his lip and peers up at Rathburton.

> CUTHBERT
> Looks like the bottom line is twelve dollars and sixty-three cents.

Rathburton frowns.

> RATHBURTON
> Really? I was hoping for a little more.

> CUTHBERT
> Nope. Sorry. It's all right here.

Cuthbert taps his paper. Rathburton sighs. Cuthbert fidgets.

> RATHBURTON
> Fine, whatever is fair.

Cuthbert blinks, then quickly opens his cash register and counts out the money. He thrusts the money and his scratch paper at Rathburton.

> CUTHBERT
> Sign here.

Rathburton signs and sticks the money in his pocket.

> RATHBURTON
> Thank you.

> CUTHBERT
> Glad to be of service. Stop by any time.

Rathburton stops at the door and looks back at the merchandise.

> RATHBURTON
> I don't think that's . . . likely.

He goes out. Cuthbert closes his eyes and breathes a sigh of relief. Then he notices the newspaper ad, grabs it, and tears it up. He snatches the phone and punches several numbers.

> CUTHBERT
> Cuthbert's Emporium. Cancel my ad. That's right. Now.

He hangs up. He looks at the scraps of the newspaper ad, then laughs in relief.

The roof BULGES downward. Lights flash and go out, and dust falls. I-beams SQUEAL. Cuthbert's eyes go large and he runs to the window, looking up.

> CUTHBERT
> No! Not here! Not here!

He screams again and runs madly back and forth through the store, grabbing an item here and there, as more dust falls and obscures everything.

> CUTHBERT (O.S.)
> No! My store! My beautiful store!

A huge CRASH echoes through the gloom.

FADE TO BLACK

MACROHARD #4

FADE IN:

INT. LIVING ROOM - DAY

A young WOMAN scurries around picking up discarded men's clothes and straightening magazines. A CRONE inspects her work.

> CRONE
> Another thing my Johnnie hates is fussing. And that so-called casserole was horrid. You really ought to dress up more. What's the matter with your hair, anyway?

The young Woman fumes, slamming down books and throwing the clothes through a doorway.

> CRONE
> I don't know why he got married so young. You'd think a son would show more sense.

The front door opens and a forty-ish MAN walks in.

> MAN
> Honey, you know the new car we couldn't afford? Come see what Mom bought me.

The Woman gapes, then pushes past to gaze out the door.

> MAN
> And she can stay another two weeks.

The crone sneers. The Woman glares from one to the other, then charges out the door.

> MAN
> Isn't it . . . the key's in . . . . Hey, be careful.

An engine ROARS, tires SQUEAL. The man looks alarmed, then dives toward the crone as the ROARING nears. With a tremendous CRASH, glass SHATTERS, beams fall, and a cloud of dust erupts, obscuring everything. SILENCE descends.

INT. STUDY

Covered in dust, the Woman pushes a beam aside and enters. Plaster falls behind her. A SIREN HOWLS in the distance.

She sits at a desk and starts a computer. She taps the desk. The SIREN nears.

> WOMAN
> Come on. Come on.

She taps some keys, and the screen glows. Words appear: "Date" and "Time." Her fingers skitter faster. After Date comes "today." After Time appears "-30 minutes."

The siren cuts off and car doors SLAM outside.

> POLICEMAN (O.S.)
> Anyone in there?

The Woman smashes her fist on the Enter key. She, her desk, and the computer dissolve in a swirl of color.

INT. LIVING ROOM - DAY

The young Woman sets down books and tosses clothes through a doorway.

> CRONE
> I don't know why he got married so young. You'd think a son would show more sense.

The front door opens and the forty-ish Man walks in.

> MAN
> Honey, you know the new car we couldn't afford? Come see what Mom bought me.

The Woman closes her eyes and smiles slowly. She glances at the crone, then grins at the man.

> WOMAN
> Certainly, dear.

They exit.

The picture fades into the logo of MACROHARD: A blacksmith with raised hammer, holding an old-fashioned computer disk with a pair of tongs over an anvil.

> NARRATOR (V.O.)
> Macrohard—the leading edge in temporal distortion software, and proud sponsor of the 1890 World's Fair.

FADE TO BLACK

O'CONNOR'S THIRD QUEST,
NOT COUNTING
THE TWO HE DIDN'T FINISH

(a.k.a.: **The Mad Orthodontist From Hell**)

His fortunes a-tumble, his stomach a-rumble,
O'Connor thought food should come first,
While high in a tower, a princess's bower,
A king knew his daughter was cursed.

"You can't keep me collared," Elizabeth hollered.
"A princess has got to be married.
And now that your wizard has dubbed me a lizard
My choices are shrinkingly varied."

"'Tis true," said the king, "for your face is a thing
That would kill any chance for a pact."
Said she, "But with money I'll get me a honey.
It's foolish relying on tact."

"Now wait," said her father, "I know it's a bother,
But royalty follows tradition."
And much as she ranted and acidly canted,
He firmly ignored her sedition.

"I've got it, my child." And slowly he smiled.
"I'll sponsor a quest to the wood.
The knight who can do in the witch is a shoo-in.
By her even you would look good."

They hired the son of old Madi. He'd won
An award for his high pressure sales.
The avenue glistened while all the knights listened
To stories of fame and travails.

"Beware," cried a raven. "'Tis best to be craven;
The princess shuns everything straight.
She should have had braces in several places,
On teeth and on brain and on fate."

But most of the fighters were sensible blighters.
They'd heard of the princess's lacks.
And soon all but one had decided to run;
O'Connor stood munching his snacks.

"A knight always eating? He'll like take a beating
And bolt," said the king in disgust.
"He's fine," said his daughter, "and once he has
fought her
The witch will be nothing but rust."

The king shook his head and departed in dread.
Elizabeth turned to the knight.
She wore a stout veil—three layers of mail—
Enough not to give him a fright.

She gave him instructions. He made his deductions
And thought the reward could be ample,
For winning her hand meant a title and land,
And elegant food he could sample.

"Since married to wealth could be good for my
health,
The option of freedom I'll rue."
Said she, "You will win with my magic-proof gin,
So buck up and earn option two."

The sky softly wept on the knight as he crept
Toward the House of Unnamable Fear.
He sniffled, "I'm bold when I'm fighting a cold,
But stalking's a pain in the rear."

His travel was thrifty. A hundred and fifty,
Near two hundred yards did he go.
He snuck beneath trees, under bushes on knees,
Then rested when rain became snow.

Come morning, resuming, the witch's hut looming,
He sidled his way to the door.
But courage near soured. Three stories it towered.
He wished of the gin he had more.

He thought of the mad orthodontist who had
Till he died made his home in this dwelling.
Then Hades apprenticed the magical dentist . . . .
The witch would seem hardly repelling.

He twisted the handle. Inside was a candle
Two feet on a side and six tall.
It looked like a coffin. Its light drifted off in
A bid to illumine the hall.

The knight bravely swallowed. A staircase he
followed.
It widdershins mounted a flight.
The larder was drab so he went to the lab;
He entered and gagged at the sight.

The innards of moose and a sacrificed goose
Played host to a party of lice,
While foul-smelling potions and twisted devotions
Suggested the witch wasn't nice.

Then screeling around came a nauseous sound,
A dentally mutated voice:
"My name is Eve Isle. En garde, for your vile
Assault was a dubious choice.

"I've captured and hidden the princess. You're bidden
To rescue the hag if you can.
I'm laying out mazes in devilish ways. Is
Your courage enough for this plan?"

O'Connor thought briefly. Deception was chiefly
The province of witches like Eve.
He'd not play the sap and get caught in her trap;
He gamely decided—to leave.

Yet back at the door he considered his chore
To be too premature to abort.
The candle's dim flame cast him flickers of shame.
To run—he just wasn't the sort.

Alternatives beckoned. He suddenly reckoned
That fire was sort of expected,
So candle he rocked until over it knocked,
And soon the whole place was infected.

While flames were seducing the house and reducing
Its secret nefarious shape,
O'Connor went seeking, and from the back sneaking
Saw princess and woman in cape.

"You're here," the knight cried. "But I thought she
had lied."
"Some rescue," Elizabeth said.
The stranger doffed cape and attacked him. "You
rape
My nice home, you hyena. You're dead!"

O'Connor just grinned for his body was gin'd,
From magic was surely preserved.
He pulled out his blade. 'Twas the wooden one made
For his practice. "Oh, damn," he observed.

Yet mighty and brave (she had nought but a stave),
He felled her his thirtieth blow.
She hit on a stump; her head grew a lump;
Her bite-plate flew out in the snow.

And then she distorted, her visage contorted.
O'Connor and princess stood gaping.
The princess yelled, "Slay!" But his blade he did stay.
Eve Isle completed reshaping.

The princess grew stormy. "You must do it for me.
Now kill this deceitful accused."
But lo, in the place of the crone lay a face
So becoming O'Connor refused.

"Not I," said O'Connor. "It brings me no honor,
For chivalry treasures a beaut'.
She may be a chiller, a cold-blooded killer,
But none of that counts if she's cute."

Then wakened Eve Isle. With disarming smile
Said, "Thank you for ending my curse.
The Bite-Plate Surprise from a dentist of lies
Made looks and demeanor perverse."

Elizabeth freaked. "Evil bite-plate?" she shrieked.
"It's you who are lying and foul."
She grabbed the retainer—they couldn't restrain
her—
And jammed it far back in her jowl.

Then suddenly, churning, the princess was turning,
Her unveiled features gone fright'ning.
Yet soon on the ground she lay slender, not round,
And pretty. The sky split with lightning.

"You fool!" came blaring, a cloud-visage glaring:
The Mad Orthodontist from Hell.
"You've ruined it. My curses are simple reverses.
I hate a beneficent spell."

He faded, now sighing, or practically crying.
Elizabeth turned to Eve Isle.
"I'm sorry we scared you, and glad that we spared
you.
Perhaps you'll come visit awhile?"

Returning and musing, O'Connor tried choosing.
"The princess is pretty and rich.
But Isle is stunning, libido is running.
I *really* prefer the ex-witch."

Then ere he selected, the princess defected.
"I'm sorry. I mean no defiance,
But now that I can I must follow Dad's plan.
I'll wed to cement an alliance."

O'Connor was gracious; her father loquacious.
But Isle shot down option three.
"So sorry," she stuttered. Her eyelashes fluttered.
"I'm not a knight person, you see."

And thus did O'Connor know love was a goner.
"A bummer. I just get the fee.
Yet—this time I finished, my fame undiminished . . . .
I wonder what's serving for tea?"

That's it. The end. All finished.

Now go do something useful, like post a scathing review online or whatever. After all, with this much variety, there must be something you didn't like.

Me, I'm outa here.

(more abuse at www.charleypearson.com)

(including an about-the-author thingy, if you're into that kind of stuff)

(This page reserved for disparaging comments
and other reader notes.)

(Plus, it often seems like a good idea
to have a blank page at the end of a book
for potential damage control.)

(Hey, we know how often you spill things.)

(Well, I do, anyway.)